# FRIENDLY FIRE

### A NOVEL

# FRIENDLY FIRE

A NOVEL

## LISA GUENTHER

NeWest
Press

Board Editor: Leslie Vermeer
Cover photo credits: nikkytok/BigStock.com & tomofbluesprings/BigStock.com
Author photo: Angela Csiki
Cover and Interior Design: Justine Ma

**Library and Archives Canada Cataloguing in Publication**
Guenther, Lisa, 1981-, author
    Friendly fire / Lisa Guenther.
(Nunatak first fiction series ; no. 42)
Issued in print and electronic formats.
ISBN 978-1-926455-41-9 (pbk.).--ISBN 978-1-926455-42-6 (epub).-- ISBN 978-1-926455-43-3 (mobi)

    I. Title. II. Series: Nunatak first fiction ; no. 42
PS8613.U4473F75 2015        C813'.6        C2015-901795-5
                                         C2015-901796-3

NeWest Press acknowledges the support of the Canada Council for the Arts, the Alberta Foundation for the Arts, and the Edmonton Arts Council for support of our publishing program. This project is funded in part by the Government of Canada.

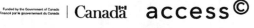

*No bison were harmed in the making of this book.*
Printed and bound in Canada
First Edition: October 2015

**NeWest Press**

No. 201, 8540 109 Street, Edmonton, Alberta  T6G 1E6
**t.**  780.432.9427  **w.**  newestpress.com

*To Mary Guenther, the first great storyteller I knew.*

# CHAPTER ONE

It's only June, but the grass in the pastures and ditches is already sunburnt and dead from the drought. Smoke hangs in the air, a constant reminder of the burning forests in the north, around Loon Lake. The water in this lake, Brightsand Lake, is lower than anyone's ever seen it. A few yards from where we sit, new rocks break the lake's surface, like seedlings emerging from the soil. I've never seen these rocks before — they've always been submerged.

Luke Cherville is leaning back in his lawn chair, his beer growing warm. Luke likes to savour his booze rather than just tip it back. His skin is already turning a deep brown, filling me with a mix of admiration and jealousy. Luke, like his sister Jen, is all high cheekbones and leanly muscled limbs. I could almost throw up. I really shouldn't complain, though, since I'm dating him.

My own fair skin is burning despite the sunscreen. I dip my floppy straw hat in the cool water and flick my bangs out of my eyes. Time for a cut.

The sun is my enemy. Not only does it roast my skin, but it makes my hair and nails grow like weeds. And it bleaches my black hair red, which is fine until the summer is over and my roots come in black again. Hence the silly grandma hat, which, though unstylish, solves both these problems.

Brightsand Lake is a large oval, and we sit on the northeast shore. A couple feet from where we lounge, cold springs bubble up from the reeds, rusting the sand and chilling the water. My Aunt Bea painted one of these springs. Soft mineral formations like aquatic cities within the springs, the tall grasses standing guard around the pools. The canvas has been hanging in her kitchen since before Mom got sick — more than five years now — but every time I look at it, I notice more details.

North of us is the main beach, a mile of golden sand dotted with people and beach blankets. On the west part of the main beach, sandbars are pushing out of the water like the ribs of a starving whale. People have planted their lawn chairs on the sandbars and lounge with their feet in the water.

I've been coming to this park for as long as I can remember. Dad and I used to ride our horses here in the early spring and late fall, when the campers weren't around. We'd take the short-cut along Crocus Ridge and through Aunt Bea and Uncle Will's pastures, gallop down the jack pine-lined fairways of the park's golf course, then follow the winding road deeper into the park, through the black spruce and poplar. When we reached the main beach, we'd stop our horses and watch, silent. Sometimes white-tailed deer would emerge from the forest, edge up to the lake for a drink. Then we'd lope down the beach, the horses' hooves flinging clumps of wet sand like kids having a food fight. Deer would startle, bound back into the woods.

In the off-season, the park was ours. But after my mom died, we stopped riding our horses here. I can't tell you why, exactly. I didn't ask Dad if he wanted to, and he didn't suggest it.

My life is divided in two. The time before my mom died, and the time after. The time before is set, like a bug stuck in hardened amber. The time after keeps growing, changing. Almost unrecognizable from the life I thought I'd have.

Today, though, I can pretend everything's as it should be. I can even imagine that Brightsand Lake Park is mine again. At least this rocky strip of beach. I dip my hat in the water again.

"Luke, I'm so hot." I sigh.

"Well, let's go out there." Luke puts his drink down, stands up.

We slide into our sandals and wade out slowly, trying not to slip on the slimy rocks. We are nearly waist deep when Luke pretends to fall. When I reach for him, he pulls me into the icy water. I squeal, come up gasping for air, blinking water out of my eyes. Luke stands back laughing at me.

"YOU SON OF A BASTARD! YOUR ASS IS GRASS, SEABASS!" I tackle him. We're both laughing as we go under again. In the struggle, I nick my left calf on a jagged rock. Luke is pushing me under, still laughing, while I watch my blood drift through the water, a thin line of rusty smoke. Fascinated, I trace its progress with my eyes. And suddenly I see it.

Floating toward us. Face down. Fishing line trails from the left leg. She's a boat gone adrift.

Long dark hair drifts like seaweed. Hides her face.

Is it her?

Not her. No. No. No.

The arms hang down. Long thin fingers. Ring finger missing. Something under the nails. Dirt? No. Paint. Dark blue.

No, no, no, no, no, no.

Two days ago. I saw her. Just saw her.

I thrash, arms smashing water.

"What the hell, Darby?" Luke says.

"Oh, God! Bea! Bea!" Run for her. Run. Help. Help her. Water slows me.

He is clutching my arm. His hands, they're strong. Holding me back. Rage hot as the sun.

"Let go! Let go! Help her! Let me — I need, she needs..."

"Darby, don't touch her. She's ... it's too late."

I'm retching into the lake. Luke's hands in my hair. Roaring. My throat burning.

Then the strangest thing happens. I'm still screaming, but I start to feel distant from myself, like a part of me is observing everything. Broken in two.

A wisp of wind stirs the cold, glassy surface of the lake. I tip my head back, howling now, like a feral dog. The sun glares down from the cloudless sky.

The heat in my body disappears. I watch the vomit slowly drift apart in the numbing water, see some of it bump against my left hip. Food for the jackfish.

We walk back to Luke's car and he calls the RCMP on his cell phone. Cell service is spotty, so he walks around until he finds a spot with good reception. I wrap myself in a worn pink beach blanket and sit on a picnic table under the pavilion, sobbing so my whole body hurts. Luke wraps his arms around me, but I'm angry at him for holding me back. I know he was right, but I can't help it. I shrug off his arms, stand. Feel sick again.

I dry heave, spit stomach acid into the pavilion's dusty gravel.

The Turtleford and St. Walburg RCMP arrive first. Luke takes them down to the beach. I watch from the table.

Luke comes back with Sergeant Cardinal. Cardinal takes our statements, asks us questions. I don't think he even knew my name before today. I try to focus on his questions, but I can't understand him. His voice is muffled, as though we're under water. Cardinal keeps repeating the questions. I think I'm answering them right, but I'm not sure.

About half an hour later a canine unit from Lloydminster pulls up. Then more RCMP from Battleford. Luke and I watch them from our perch under the pavilion. They park their cars next to the ball diamonds. Set up barricades blocking off the dirt trail that runs up and around the pavilion. Groups of cops follow the path down to the lake while others move toward the boat launch. I wonder what they're doing at the boat launch. What are they looking for? I want to know every detail.

Sergeant Cardinal says the cops from Saskatoon will want to interview us. We can wait for them here or at the station in Turtleford. Major Crimes, he calls them.

Bea is the victim of a Major Crime. A Major Crime victim. A victim.

Her body is floating in the lake. But that can't be my aunt. It's not Bea. I just saw her two days ago. She looked happy. How can she be dead?

Sometimes when Bea smiles, her eyes still look tired. Last time I saw her, though, smile lines crinkled up all around her eyes as soon as she got out of her car. Something was different.

"What's up?" I asked her. I was unsaddling Bucky, my horse, by the barn.

"What do you mean?"

"I don't know. You just look really happy," I said, then regretted it. Regretted bringing up her sadness.

She stopped smiling for a moment. The crinkles around her eyes disappeared and her whole face went blank. Neutral. Like she was hiding her tells.

"I wanted to give you this." She handed me a large rectangular package wrapped in brown paper. A painting.

"Can I open it?"

"Not yet. Wait until I'm gone." She stroked the white blaze on Bucky's face, rubbed his sweaty neck. "He's a beautiful colour. Such a rich, burnt red. I should do a portrait of you and Bucky sometime."

"Sure. That would be great."

She hugged me hard then. "I love you, sweetie," she whispered in my ear.

She let go of me, looked around the yard, and slid into her car. Then she was gone.

I didn't have a chance to open the package until the end of the day. It was an oil painting of my mom as a young woman, mounted on a black horse. She was wearing some kind of men's military jacket, brown with swatches of red on the shoulders and collar. The jacket was a little too big for her, but she looked fantastic, like some sort of warrior. It took me a moment to realize the horse was Magic.

Mom and Bea were both barrel racers, and Magic propelled Mom to many victories, including a Calgary Stampede championship sometime in the 1970s. Bea rode Cash, a full brother to Magic. Both horses were born on Grandpa's ranch, sired by Faux Pas, a former RCMP stud.

Magic was fast, smart, and mean. When I was a toddler, she ran right over top of me, knocked out two of my baby teeth with her hoof. Later I was forbidden to ride her. But when I was thirteen, I managed to lure her into a halter with oats, saddle her, and swing myself into the saddle as she danced around. As soon as my butt hit the saddle, Magic bolted from the yard, running north. We ripped up the fireguard and raced down deer trails through the provincial forest for hours. On the way home, Magic still pulled on the bit, wanting to run. When a grouse exploded from the brush beside us, she reared up, then lunged forward into a full gallop again. I wasn't able to stop her until we came to a clearing. I pulled the left rein, easing her into a sweeping turn. Together we circled the clearing over and over. Eventually she slowed enough for me to pull her into tight circles, her nose nearly touching my boot. I kept disengaging her hip, making her hind legs cross, until she seemed calm. White lather streaked her neck, and I was soaked in sweat, too.

Magic was exhilaration tipping into terror.

The second time I tried to sneak a ride, I was daydreaming about the ride ahead as I saddled her up, still daydreaming when I swung my leg over the saddle. Magic bucked me off before my right foot was in the stirrup. I broke my collarbone, and Magic shattered my belief that we shared some sort of telepathic bond.

Mom was furious.

Months after my collarbone healed, I rode Magic again.

But Mom or Dad always rode with me, coaching me if Magic started acting up. Magic taught me to focus. If she caught me daydreaming, she would just as soon throw me into a pile of deadfall as do anything else.

The year after Mom died, Magic broke her leg. Dad found her and had to put her down. I cried as hard for that horse as I did for my mother.

The portrait was so detailed that it was almost like having Mom and Magic in the room with me. I propped it up on the dresser across from my bed so it would be the first thing I saw in the morning.

Luke says he'll talk to Cardinal about us leaving. He says we should wait at my house for Major Crimes to show up. It's only a few miles away anyway.

I tell him it's okay. I don't want to go home. I don't want this in my house. I want it here, contained, not spreading into the rest of my life like cancer.

As long as I stay here, I can tell myself that it's a mistake. I'll pretend it's an episode of *Law and Order*. A really weird episode, set in rural Saskatchewan. Or maybe we're by the Hudson River. If I look toward the lake and don't think about it, I can sort of pretend it's the Hudson River. Any second now Benson and Stabler will pull up. They'll look at the crime scene, talk to the medical examiner. Then one of them will say something cheesy, and I'll cringe.

I wonder if real cops make awful jokes. Are they doing that right now? Joking about my aunt?

I go through the potential suspects in my mind. Usually it's someone the victim knows, but I can't imagine anyone I know doing this. It could be a chance encounter. A serial killer or something. There are a lot of sick people out there. "Out there" being far away from here.

Except it is here. It's happening here.

What if it's someone I know? What happens then?

Fuck, fuck, fuck. I don't even want to fucking think about it. I can't deal with this bullshit.

If Bea was here, she'd smile at me and tell me we would be okay.

"Cowboy up, Buttercup."

And I would do it, because she has this way of making me believe I'm strong enough to get through anything.

Bea is different from everyone else in my family. Was different. She listened to me. My mom didn't really listen. My mom talked at me.

When I was a kid, my dad and I were inseparable, but he doesn't really see me anymore. Maybe fathers always grow distant as their daughters grow up.

Dad taught me how to ride. Mom was a good rider, too, maybe even better than he was. But she was impatient. She'd give me so many instructions at once that I could never keep anything straight.

"I don't have time for this," she'd say every time I made a mistake. "How many times do I have to tell you?"

"She's the cow that can't remember when she was a calf," Dad used to say, making me giggle. Then, "Don't tell her I said that."

Dad also used to say that there are three types of people in the world. Men, women, and band singers. I think that's a Stan Kenton quote. Anyway, Dad started telling me about the three types of people when Bea realized that I could sing.

Looking back, it shouldn't have been a big surprise that I

could sing. Dad played guitar in cover bands for years. At one time, he played at almost every wedding dance in this part of Saskatchewan. Grandma Swank, Dad's mother, still teaches piano and sings in the choir at the Four Square Church at Turtle Lake. Mom loved music even though she didn't know how to sing. She always said she'd never had time to learn how to sing, but she loved Johnny Cash and Ian and Sylvia Tyson.

Bea loved music too. She told me once that when she listened to music, she saw colours. Like one of those hippie light shows they used to put on at rock concerts. I've never seen colours the way Bea does, but I kind of see the songs. Little movies. One song, "Twist the Knife," by Neko Case, makes me think of fancy young women in ball gowns waltzing with wolf men.

Bea used to babysit me when Mom worked days. I loved to watch her paint. Sometimes she'd let me paint on her white smock while she was wearing it.

One winter day we were in her studio, Bea working on a landscape and me drawing stick pictures of the pony I wanted for my fifth birthday. Bea often hummed along with the radio while she worked. It must have been the anniversary of Buddy Holly's death because the DJ played the long version of "American Pie." Bea put down her paint-covered knife, pulled me away from my chair, and danced with me. She sang every word of that song. A little flat. She was always a little flat. Mom tended to be sharp.

After hearing the chorus once, I knew it too and started singing along.

Toward the end of the song, Bea stopped singing and watched me. When the song was over, she lifted me onto a table and asked me to sing the chorus again. I took a deep breath and sang as loud as I could. When I reached the chorus, I paused.

"Aunty Bea, what's a levee?"

"It's like a dam, sweetie. Keep singing."

When I finished, she said, "Darby, you have a real voice."

Dad picked me up a couple hours later, and Bea had me sing for him. By that time, she'd taught me three of the verses. Dad didn't even let me finish before he picked me up and hugged me so hard I started crying. He wiped the tears off my cheeks with his thumb and drove me straight to Grandma Swank's house.

Grandma listened to me sing, then said, "She better start with piano lessons. Bring her over tomorrow." Grandma was always strict with me, and I had been a little scared of her before I started music lessons. But even at that age I worked hard at my lessons. I wanted to be a piano teacher like Grandma, or maybe even a musician like Joni Mitchell. I was determined to get my Grade Eight in piano, to learn everything I could about music.

After a few years, Grandma started bringing me to choir practices at the Turtle Lake Mission. They always had a pretty rocking choir. Lots of energy. The Christmas carols were my favourite, especially "Silent Night."

But as I got older, Mom started to push back against my music. I think that was partly Grandma's fault because she badmouthed Mom all the time. Called her a Cossack, once, right in front of me. When I asked Mom what a Cossack was, she was furious. She phoned Grandma right away. The argument with Grandma ended when Mom yelled, "I am not raising her as a heathen, Jolene. She's never even seen an Orthodox church. Jesus Christ, I've never even seen an Orthodox Church. Excuse me? I will take the Lord's name in vain any time I want to, but I will not tolerate you calling me names in front of my child. Do it again and you won't see her anymore." She slammed down the phone.

I don't blame Mom for being pissed at Grandma. Grandma's overbearing. But then, so was Mom sometimes. They were two soloists fighting for the best part.

Mom was the best cook in the neighbourhood, and Grandma Swank was jealous. Mom always said she'd better be the best cook with all the practice she'd had. Her own mother died shortly after giving birth to my Uncle Henry. As the oldest, Mom stepped into her mother's shoes. Cooking, cleaning, packing lunches, bossing her younger siblings around — though somehow I imagine she was born bossy. She was eleven when that happened.

Mom could be nurturing, like most mothers, I guess. She used to make chocolate chip cookies for me every Sunday morning, right up until she got sick. I'd help her measure and mix the ingredients, and she pretended not to see me steal spoonfuls of the raw cookie dough. I'd watch the cookies bake, becoming more and more impatient as the smell of vanilla and chocolate filled the house.

It doesn't matter if you're seven or fourteen or forty-seven, homemade cookies are always divine.

But when she got into a mood, she was hard on me. She was worse as I got older, and it grew difficult to remember the other side of her. It was as if the kind version of Mom didn't exist a lot of the time. She could make me feel two inches tall. Nothing I did was good enough.

We had a really bad fight when I was fourteen. I'd flunked another math quiz.

"How the fuck are you going to get into university with these grades?" she yelled, waving the quiz in my face. I can still see the red F scrawled at the top of the page.

"I'm in grade nine, Mom. Relax." Nervous, but I didn't want her to see that. Couldn't let her see any weakness. I sat down at the kitchen table and picked up my acoustic guitar, a beautiful Tacoma that Dad had given me for my twelfth birthday. I was trying not to provoke her, but I didn't know what to say.

"*That* is the problem. That fucking guitar. No wonder you're so stupid." She yanked the guitar from my hands.

"Give it back!"

"No. No more fucking music until you pull up your fucking marks."

"What? No! Give it back! I don't even want to go to university!"

"What did you just say?"

"I don't care about school!"

"Well, you better learn to care. Because the only way you're getting that guitar back is if you bring up your shitty grades. And if you're too much of a retard to manage that, I'll burn your fucking guitar." She stomped toward her room, guitar in hand.

Sheer horror. She would do it, too. Then, an epiphany.

"Whatever. I'll still be able to sing."

Even as I was saying it, I knew I'd made a mistake. Mom stopped, her body as rigid as a dead poplar.

"What?"

"Nothing."

She turned around. Her right eye twitched twice.

"Nothing, nothing. I'll study. I'll do better." Begging now.

Mom lifted the guitar above her head, smashed it against the kitchen table. The guitar splintered against the solid oak.

"No! No!" I jumped up, reached for the strings that used to make my fingers bleed. The frets that used to feel too wide for my fingers but now fit perfectly.

But it was too late. Mom smashed it again and again. Splinters all over the linoleum floor. Each time the guitar hit the table, I could feel the impact reverberate through my whole body.

Without a word, I walked out the door, down the driveway, and across the road.

Aunt Bea took me in without any questions. Uncle Will and Dad were at some cow seminar, so we had a girls' night. We watched *Cat on a Hot Tin Roof,* one of our faves. We could recite the lines along with the characters on screen. I would be Brick, and Bea would be Maggie. Or she would play Big Daddy and me Gooper.

Brick could never be what his family wanted — straight. I could never be what my mother wanted — smart and sweet.

Even though the next day was a school day, Bea let me sleep in. When I finally got up, she was making scrambled eggs and salsa, breakfast sausage, and toast.

I loved everything about Bea's kitchen. The mismatched china, the bluebells and daisies that dropped their petals on the table. Buffalo beans in the early spring. Yellow walls and worn fir floors. Dishes in the sink. Everything in Mom's kitchen was matchy-matchy and so clean and tidy I was afraid to drop a crumb on the floor.

As we both sat down to eat, Bea took a long sip of coffee, then spoke.

"You know, Darby, your mom loves you very much."

"Yeah, right," I snorted. "She hates me. She's a psycho."

"No, she loves you. She just worries herself sick about you. That's her problem. She worries too much about everything, things she can't control. That's why she gets so mad at you sometimes."

"Well, I don't care. She treats me like a dog she can kick. I'm sick of it." I shovelled a forkful of egg into my mouth, chewing quickly. "Can I move in with you? Just 'til I'm done school."

Bea choked on her coffee.

"Honey, I'm sorry. I'd love to have you here, but you can't live with us."

"Why not?"

"Because you have two parents who love you very much right across the road. Now finish your breakfast and get ready for school. I'm driving you in."

"Bea, please. Don't make me go back home."

"Darby, I'll talk to your mother, but you need to learn to live together. Now go jump in the shower. You smell like a barnyard."

When I got off the bus that day, Mom's eyes were red from crying. She apologized and wrapped me in a hug, something she hadn't done for months. After that, things were better. Mom was still strict, and we still argued, but there were no more knockdown, all-out screaming matches. Sometimes Mom would get this strained look on her face, as though she were holding something back, but she never called me names again.

Sometimes I wonder what Bea might have said to Mom.

"May, you're hurting your daughter."

"May, you suck as a mother. Smarten up."

"May, you have to treat Darby like a human being. You can't control her every move. If you try to hold on too tight, you'll lose her. You'll fail. You're failing now."

When Mom died two years later, we were on pretty good terms. And we had Aunt Bea to thank for that.

Major Crimes is here. They want to ask us questions. Luke walks off with one of them. He's an older guy, grey hair, slight pot-belly, but strong looking. His neck is thicker than my thigh.

I stay on the picnic bench with the other one. A tall woman, maybe forty, maybe older. Back ramrod straight. Ash-blonde hair shaped into a pixie cut. Says her name is Sergeant Steele.

Why would her parents name her Sergeant? I wonder stupidly, then almost laugh when I get it.

She pulls out a voice recorder, recites the date, my name, our location. Her voice is so soft I have to listen closely to hear her. Straining like that makes me tense. I need a smoke.

"Hey, um, I hate to ask, but can I bum a smoke off you?"

She frowns at me. "I don't smoke."

She's lying; I can smell it on her. But I don't ask again.

"Bea Fletcher was your aunt?"

"Yes." Aunt. One word to sum up a life-long relationship.

"She's married?"

"Yes." Steele already knows that, so why would she ask? She asks me a whole bunch of other useless questions, too. She's trying to look casual, but she's watching me so closely I feel like a criminal. Eventually she circles back to my uncle.

"Will Fletcher is your uncle."

"Yes." I think I hesitated before I said it. I wonder if she noticed. The truth is Will is also my dad's cousin. His dad was my Grandma Swank's brother. Everyone who lives around here knows that. But I don't like to tell outsiders because they'll think we're inbred hicks.

"Did Bea and Will ever argue?"

What kind of question is that? Everyone must argue sometimes. But I don't want to get Will in trouble for no reason. Especially with Steele. Despite her gentle voice, I'm on high alert. Maybe it's her name. Maybe it's her neutral face, hiding the way she feels about me and my family. She barely seems human, I think.

"No. Will was good to her. He really took care of her when she needed him." Uncle Will was always sweet to Bea when she was sick. He'd make her a pot of tea, even buy her flowers. He's the only man I know around here who bought his wife flowers several times a year.

"What do you mean? Was she sick?"

"She got a lot of headaches. Multi-day migraines."

"Did she get hurt? Broken bones, sprains, that kind of thing?"

"She got bucked off a few colts. Broke her wrist a couple times, I think."

Steele raises her eyebrows very slightly. For a moment, her green eyes hold sorrow, but then it's gone. I wonder why that comment would raise emotion.

She asks me several more questions about the wrecks Bea had with her horses. I realize I don't know very much about the accidents. I've never seen her get bucked off, just the results afterwards.

"She certainly had a lot of horse riding accidents, didn't she?" says Steele.

She thinks Bea was a crap rider, I think. What the hell does she know? Probably can't tell a horse's ass from its ears.

"She started colts, you know. That's why she got hurt so

much. Anyone would. She was a good rider." My voice is strident. I must sound defensive. But Steele is still perfectly composed. Detached.

"Were they happy, your aunt and uncle?"

"Yeah, I guess." Steele just looks at me. "Well, I mean, I think Bea looked a little sad sometimes, but I thought it was because they couldn't have children."

"Why couldn't they have children?"

"I don't know. I didn't ask. I don't actually know that they couldn't have children, I guess."

"Why would you think that?"

"Everyone around here has kids."

"Why wouldn't they adopt, then?"

"I don't know. You'll have to ask them. I mean, Will." Throat closes up. "Are you sure you don't have a smoke? I could really use one."

Steele stares at me, and then she drops the clinical façade. She reaches into her bag, offers me a pack of Canadian Classics. I light a smoke, give her a weak smile.

"Tom Thomson died this way, you know. In a lake, with fishing line wrapped around his leg. He was one of Bea's favourite artists." I take a long drag. "They never figured out who killed him."

"Darby, did Bea seem different lately?"

"What do you mean?"

"Did she seem worried? Did she say or do anything out of the ordinary that made you think she was worried?"

"No. I just saw her two days ago, and she seemed really happy." I tell her about Bea's visit.

"Was there anything about that visit that was unusual?"

"No." I stop, think. "Well, I wondered for a moment if she was going somewhere."

"What made you think that?"

"It was just that she hugged me so hard. Like she wouldn't

see me for a while."

And then it hits me. Maybe she was leaving. Maybe she was saying goodbye. But why?

I sob now. Steele turns off the voice recorder and says that if I remember anything else, I should talk to Sergeant Cardinal in Turtleford.

I close my eyes, shut out everything around me. Travel deeper and deeper inside myself, past the denial and shock, past memory, until I am alone with my grief. A stone worn smooth by water. Hard and cold, but small enough that I can carry it wherever I go.

# CHAPTER TWO

The next morning, I stumble out of my bedroom at seven o'clock. I half-expect to see Steele and Cardinal sitting at the kitchen table. I dreamed they grilled me about Bea while Dad made omelets.

*Tell us who killed her, Darby. Tell us. Was it you? Was it your dad? We know you know.*

They hissed like snakes, and when I cried, the hissing grew louder and louder, until it was a shriek, then a train whistle. Then it was my alarm, and I woke up soaked in sweat.

Dad's already making breakfast — mushroom omelets and hash browns, just like Mom used to make it. Except he always adds a spoonful of salsa on the side.

Before Mom got sick, Dad could barely boil water. At first, he took over the kitchen duties so she could rest, so he could help her beat the leukemia. After she was gone, he could have fallen into bachelor mode, living off pork and beans or coercing me into doing all the cooking. Grandma Swank even offered to move in with us for a while, to take care of us. But instead, Dad and I divvied up supper duties. I cooked twice a week, and he covered the other days.

We often cooked supper together, though. I liked making supper with Dad because he was always a little more talkative while he cooked. As though the cooking distracted him from his own quietness. I didn't know the story of how he met Mom until after she died.

"Our drummer, Marvin O'Connor, had a cousin in Maple Creek who was getting married. So we went down there to play at the wedding dance.

"The dance was in an old log barn way up in the hills, south of town. Not too far from Fort Walsh, actually. It was hot as hell, and even with all the doors open and a breeze blowing through, the barn was cooking. But everyone was dancing. Old people, young people, little kids standing on their parents' feet, learning to foxtrot while we played the old-time stuff. And then we started into the Texas swing, and everyone was getting real tight.

"After the first set, we took a rye break. And Marvin, of course, got into a fight with some cowboy, so we all went rolling outside. The cowboy Marv was fighting was a young kid — turned out he was only sixteen — but he was big and tough, and I'd have thought he was twenty at least. And he was pounding Marv, and I was thinking I'd better step in before Marv got really hurt.

"But just as I was about to jump in, this tall, black-haired cowgirl marched right in there, her spurs jingling."

At this point in Dad's story, I knew the cowgirl was my mom. She's the only person I've known who'd wear spurs to a dance and pull it off, not look like a poser.

"Nobody tried to stop her — they parted like the Red Sea. And she walked right up to that kid, grabbed his ear lobe, and dragged him out of there like he was a five-year-old boy, not a six-three monolith. He was saying, 'I'm sorry, May, just let me go, May, I won't do it again.' And she didn't say a word, but her eyes were fire, and the crowd parted again."

"The fighter was your Uncle George, by the way."

I was floored. I'd never thought of cheerful Uncle George as a scrapper. I wasn't at all surprised that Mom would wade into a fight like that, though, especially if one of her younger siblings was involved. Whenever people tell stories about my mom, they use words like *firecracker*.

Dad told that story only once and never answered any of my questions afterwards. The door was shut.

But I read Mom's cookbook like a book of short stories. In the summer, I'd sit in the verandah, sipping cold beer and writing out grocery lists as I flipped pages.

The cookbook is really a large binder, full of clippings and handwritten recipes Mom slipped into plastic page protectors to keep them clean. There's a whole section of traditional recipes that she'd learned from Great-Grandma Kolchak. That's where the cabbage soup and borscht came from. And the little pastries stuffed with sautéed mushrooms and onions.

Another section was dedicated to Grandma Kolchak's recipes. These were all in Grandma's flowery handwriting. Fruitcake, saskatoon pie, gooseberry jam, Scottish oat cakes. Grandma had added notes. *Remember to run bowl under cold water before you start the pastry. This is the fruitcake Mother made for my wedding.*

Mom had added notes in her small, neat printing. Which ingredients could be substituted or dropped. What needed to be altered in the bread recipes so the bread rose properly at our elevation. And one note that said *Tell Darby that this is the chocolate cake I made for her birthday every year.*

Sometimes, when no one's around, I lug the binder into the attic and cry over those little notes. Thank God for the page protectors.

After Mom died, some of the recipes were lost. They were still in the book, of course, but we never got the hang of them. The mushroom pastries, for example. Some vital detail must be missing from the book. Or the homemade wines that Mom and Bea made together every fall. Chokecherry, rhubarb, saskatoon berry. Bea said she couldn't get the acid levels right without Mom's help, even with the written instructions.

But sometimes I think Bea stopped making the wine because she missed Mom too much.

Dad's omelets are just as good as Mom's, though. Dad likes to use the wild mushrooms that pop up in the fields after it's rained. The wild mushrooms used to make Mom nervous — it was years before she'd even try them. By the time I was old enough to appreciate mushrooms, Mom trusted Dad enough to add his mushrooms to salads, omelets, and sauces.

Sometimes my grief for my mother is still so raw that it catches me by surprise, like trying to swallow when you've got strep throat. This is one of those mornings. I try not to think too much. Turn my brain off. Eat in silence while Dad reads *Maclean's*. Finish breakfast, help Dad clean up.

Fat pouches hang below Dad's eyes. I wonder what time he got away from the cop shop. I must have fallen asleep sometime after two a.m., and he still wasn't home.

Dad and I are drinking coffee in the verandah, trying to keep Fluffy, the barn cat, from crawling into our laps, when I hear a car snorting its way up our driveway.

"Sounds like Jenny's here," Dad says as he stands up to turf Fluffy back outside. Jen's old brown Honda races into our yard, stalls, and stops in front of the house, and Jen Cherville, my best friend since grade one, bounds up the steps. Jen has two speeds — zero or one hundred miles an hour.

"Hey, Darby, would you mind coming with me to your uncle's place? Mom's been cooking and baking ever since we heard about ... well ..." Jen stumbles over her words, pushes a piece of honey-coloured hair out of her face. "I could use some help delivering the casseroles and cookies."

I hesitate. Last time I saw Jen, she would hardly say a word to me. Like she was mad at me. I have a feeling it has something to do with her brother, Luke, but I'm not sure. You'd think Luke was her little brother, instead of two years older, the way she protects him. I don't want to deal with her today, but I can't see a way out of it.

"How much stuff do you have to carry in?"

"Lots. Me and Mom must've made eight trips loading my car. Do you mind helping carry it in?"

"Okay, sure, no problem."

The back seat of the Honda is stacked with dozens of containers. Lasagna, tuna casserole, something with a creamy sauce. Five containers of ginger snaps. Bea's favourite cookie. The food completely blocks the rear window. I look at Jen.

"I told you it was a lot. Mom gets a little obsessive about cooking every time anyone within a hundred miles dies — it's annoying." Jen puts her hand over her mouth, as though she's trying to catch the words that have spilled out. "Sorry."

"'S okay," I mumble, even though my stomach suddenly feels like it's eating itself.

Our driveway is half a mile long. When we reach the grid road, Jen slows down, glances north and south for traffic, then zips straight across the road to Will and Bea's driveway.

This driveway is at least three-quarters of a mile, lined on each side by poplar and white spruce. Jen drives slowly now, watching for deer and moose.

The driveway widens into a large yard, and Jen rolls to a stop. The house is actually a renovated church, perched on top of a small hill. The church has always seemed welcoming to me. I think it's all the wood. But today something seems amiss. Maybe it's because Bea's garden, at the bottom of the hill, is already wilted and dying. Maybe it's because the front of the church, the side facing us, looks like a face. Two arched windows high up like eyes. The wide patio door a gaping mouth. The church is staring down at us like a dumb, angry giant. I never noticed the face before today.

The hair on my arms stands up.

We haul the first load of food to the deck, and I knock on the sliding patio doors. Wilson, Bea's old shepherd-cross, is lying under a patio chair. He thumps his tail twice but doesn't get up. His black muzzle is turning grey. I didn't notice that before today, either.

Hard to believe he's the same dog he was a couple weeks ago. Crashing through the bush after rabbits and scrambling around our horses' legs, startling Bea's green-broke colt into bolting, then bucking.

"Wilson's the best thing for desensitizing horses," Bea said, grinning, after pulling her colt's head around.

I pat my leg, trying to tempt Wilson over for pets, but he doesn't budge. Jen knocks again. No answer.

"He must be checking cows," I say to Jen. She nods. Will is always checking the cows. Making sure they have enough pasture, checking that the water pumps are working, fixing fences. A big job, especially since he and Dad have about three hundred commercial cattle, plus about a hundred purebred Black Angus. And thirty broodmares and two studs.

When Uncle Will's not fixing fences and riding pasture, he's checking the markets, reading business stuff. Dad's always saying that other people could take a lesson from Will, as he's built the ranch up through sweat and business sense.

Dad doesn't give himself much credit, though I don't know why. He works just as hard, even though he's not as good with the business end. But no one knows bloodlines and genetics like Dad. I could explain *hybrid vigour* and *outcrossing* to my teachers by the time I was seven.

I slide the door open and carry the food into the kitchen, plunking it on the Arborite table. The smell of bleach, mixed with cigarette smoke, almost knocks me over.

A fat black fly buzzes around my head. I swat at it. Miss. It retreats across the room. That's when I realize that Bea's painting of Brightsand Springs is missing from the north wall of her kitchen. A rectangle of yellow paint, much darker than the surrounding wall, marks the spot where it hung.

Bea has only been gone a few days and already her house is changing.

Jen and I move into the living room. Light glints through the stained-glass windows, highlighting the back of a dark wooden rocking chair. Suddenly the rocking chair seems to buck, and Will is balancing unsteadily on his feet. The fly floats around the thin tufts of blond hair on his bullet-shaped head, and he swipes at it like a bear swatting a honeybee. He leans against the wall, and for a moment I think he's drunk. But when he speaks, his voice is clear and quiet.

"You girls startled me," he says, blinking slowly. When he looks at me, his eyes are raw and red. He doesn't hold my gaze for more than a few seconds before he's staring at his feet, as though his grey socks hold all the answers.

I hear the swish of the patio door. Jen is retreating already, under the pretense of hauling more food in. She's always been the kind of person with a comeback for any insult, but even short silences unravel her.

"We brought you some food, Uncle Will. Lena made it."

"That's good. Lena's always been a good cook."

Will shuffles to the kitchen table, slowly lowers himself into a chair. Sits there with his head in his hands, staring at the wild rose petals that have dropped onto the blue tabletop.

A flush of whiskers covers his usually clean-shaven face like weeds invading a garden. His skin, normally flushed from the sun and wind, is grey.

He is ruined, I think. He won't ever be right again.

Uncle Will's never quiet like this. At dances and parties, he always has a group of people clustered around, listening to his jokes and stories. He can tell the same story a hundred times and still make it funny by changing the pace a little or throwing in a few new details. Like his story about the time he was riding with my Grandpa Kolchak in the Cypress Hills, and Grandpa stopped to drink from a crick (Grandpa always says *crick*, not *creek*). And as they rode upstream, they found a bloated cow lying dead in the crick. Will said it smelled like a skunk stuffed with sauerkraut and left in the sun. And Grandpa turned green and said, "Well, I thought that crick tasted off."

I have no idea if that story is actually true, or how much of it's true, but everyone roars no matter how many times they've heard it.

As Jen hauls in the rest of the food, I stack the baking on the counter and the casseroles in the deep freeze.

"Let's go," Jen hisses.

I nod, and we walk quietly toward the patio door. Just as my hand touches the patio door, I look back at my uncle and hesitate.

I glance at Jen. She slides her eyes at the door.

"Uncle Will, have you eaten lately?"

Will looks at me, then rubs his face, as though I've asked a very deep question.

"No," he says.

"Do you want some breakfast?"

Jen is glaring at me.

"If it's not too much trouble," Will says. "I'm sure you girls have plans."

"Not really," I reply.

Will and Bea have always liked coffee so strong you could stand a spoon up in it. I heap several tablespoons into the coffee filter, then dig through the fridge.

The coffee smell seems to revive Will a little. Once it's done brewing, he pours three cups and even sets out milk and sugar for Jen. She adds a teaspoon of sugar and lots of two-percent milk. Will and I take it black. I slurp the deadly stuff as I scramble eggs.

Will's asking Jen about her parents, whether her dad has enough pasture for their bison. When I set the plate of eggs in front of him, he eats so fast that I'm afraid he'll choke.

Strange to be taking care of him now. It doesn't seem that long ago that he was helping me pick out and fit my 4-H calves. Uncle Will always tried to treat me like an adult. Jen, too. He always gave it to us straight.

Like the time we were both being bullied by these other girls. Me because I was an awkward grade seven girl, Jen because her dad was the vice-principal and, in Elle Kirchner's words, "a dirty Indian."

Racist bitch. Not that I had the guts to say it to her face. Jen did, though, and it made things worse.

We both dreaded walking into our homeroom every morning. Elle lived in town, and she and her sidekick, Bailey, would get to school extra early to scrawl nasty things about us on the chalkboard.

Every morning Jen and I raced to the chalkboard to erase the slurs before Mr. Nikeva, our homeroom teacher, tumbled into the classroom. Nikeva was always somehow balancing a travel mug of coffee atop a stack of binders and books and files. He was one of my favourite teachers, and sometimes I thought about telling him what was going on. He would have believed me, and he would have tried to stop it. But I couldn't bring myself to repeat the poisoned words, to share my shame.

*Darby's cunt stinks like dead fish.*

How special.

We didn't bother telling our parents. My parents didn't believe in victims. It wasn't naïveté; they'd both had hard childhoods that maimed some of their siblings into adulthood. But they saw victimhood as a choice, just as they saw every other life circumstance as a choice. That was how they'd survived, and I could never fault them for it.

And so I couldn't bother them with something that might seem trivial, like Elle Kirchner. Besides, they'd find it hard to believe that Elle was that mean. She came from a good family.

Jen's parents were more understanding of life's nuances, but even though her dad was the vice-principal, we didn't think he could help us. It's not like he could have expelled Elle.

So we decided not to tell any adults. We decided to take Luke's advice: let the storm pass.

But while we were picking out 4-H calves from the purebred herd that fall, Will overheard us licking our wounds.

"There's only one way to deal with a bully, girls. Humiliate her."

"Well, how do we do that?" Jen asked.

"Find out what makes her proud, or what she loves. Or what she wants. Find out what makes her weak and use it against her."

I had no idea what to do with this advice, but Jen did. Her tongue flicked over her lips like a cat licking the last bit of cream, and I knew she was scheming.

She waited and watched.

Elle was always flirting with Gary Weaver, the most popular guy — and the biggest dick — in school. Gary was good-looking, and lots of girls flirted with him, but Elle practically threw herself at his feet.

That October, I was at the school dance, trying to hide against the wall. I hated the music at these things, but my friends made me come. None of the guys wanted to dance with me anyway, except Luke, probably because he felt sorry for me.

Luke was pulling me to the dance floor when Jen snatched my other hand and dragged me into the bathroom.

"What are you doing?" I tried to pull my hand free, but her grip was too strong.

"You have to see this," she said.

Elle was hugging a toilet, puking her guts out. Two of her friends were laughing and trying to hold her hair back. They were laughing so hard they kept falling over. To this day, I can't smell gin without seeing Elle puking in the gym washroom.

Right after that, we watched Gary Weaver lead Elle out of the gym.

As the dance floor lights flashed across Jen's face, I saw that she was smiling.

On Monday, a rumour snaked through the school about Elle.

People whispered that she'd "done it" with Gary and a couple other guys from the hockey team, one after another, in an empty classroom. And because Gary and his two buddies were dicks, they were only too happy to brag it up.

Like most good rumours, it probably had a seed of truth in it. She maybe did have sex with Gary, or was raped by Gary, though I never knew for sure. The truth never came out, or never reached my ears. And even if it had, I wouldn't have known what to do with it. I didn't really understand the meaning behind words like *rape* or *sexual assault* in grade seven. *Consent* wasn't even in my vocabulary.

Elle hid behind her big bangs that morning, her eyes focused firmly on the floor, or her books or any space where she didn't have to meet anyone's eyes.

Jen couldn't hide her snarky smile. At first I just thought she was enjoying Elle's fall from grace. But when I saw her whispering to Bailey, Elle's former best friend, after first class, I realized who was spreading the rumours. I decided to confront her at our lockers, before English class.

"Jen, what are you doing?" I whispered behind my Steinbeck novel, hoping no one would hear or lip-read. "Why are you spreading shit about Elle?"

"I'm just reporting what I saw, Darby. Besides, what do you care? She would've done the same to us, or worse. I did this for both of us."

That was true, I thought. But it didn't make what Jen was doing right. I didn't say anything, though. I just watched.

After that, Jen was the virgin queen and Elle was the school bicycle, as in everyone had a ride. I found myself hanging out with the cool kids by default. A couple months later, Jen let Elle into our clique, but all it took was one glare to remind Elle of her place on the social ladder.

And after that, I was always glad Jen was my best friend, because I'd hate to have her as an enemy.

Uncle Will and his grown-up advice. I wonder what he would've thought of the outcome of that little pearl of wisdom.

And now here we were, treating him like a child.

"More coffee, Uncle Will?" He nods and I fill his cup, quickly and cleanly. No one pours coffee as expertly as I do.

Will finishes chewing his last bite of toast. "Darby, I hear you're back together with Luke Cherville. Good for you — you won't do any better than that boy." Will looks over at Jen. "Maybe you and Jenny here'll be sisters someday."

Jen bites her bottom lip.

Did I mention my Uncle Will has no filter? Classic extrovert.

Once Will finishes his second cup of coffee, he tells us he needs to get to work. "Need to fix fence," he says.

Jen stands up fast and pushes her chair back into the table. It screeches against the fir floor. She waves to Will with one hand as she herds me out the door. We practically run to the car.

"Awkward," Jen says as she starts her car.

"Yeah, well, how do you expect him to act when his wife's just died?" I snap.

"Okay, sorry, sorry. My bad. Look, do you want to come hang out at the cabin? My cousins went back to Saskatoon yesterday, so it's all ours. If I go home, Mom's gonna make me clean out the fridge or something."

"I guess."

She is, after all, my best friend. We are bound by our shared history.

Jen's car rattles as we speed down the gravel road, a line of dust marking our escape.

Jen's family's cabin is beach front at Horseshoe Bay, on the northwest part of Turtle Lake. The cabin is a modest A-frame, with a kitchen, a bathroom, two tiny bedrooms downstairs, and a third bedroom in a loft. The Horseshoe, the restaurant where I work, is a two-minute walk from here. Often I close up the restaurant and walk straight to this cabin, to party with Jen and our friends until four in the morning. Or to spend the night with Luke.

Jen and I are lounging on the deck, watching a man in a boat reel in a fish.

"Do you think that's a jackfish?" I ask.

Jen doesn't answer.

"Must be a jackfish," I say. "Looks too big to be anything else."

"Of course it's a jack. What else would it be?" Jen snickers. Sometimes she has this way of talking that grates on my nerves. Jen's a triple threat — smart, beautiful, and athletic. I've always been her sidekick. The one who didn't get the grades in high school, who warmed the bench during volleyball games. Flunked out of university before the first semester was up, while she earned scholarships left and right and got accepted into law school.

For a while after I left university, Jen called me Grad, as in Christmas Grad, until I got drunk and told her to fuck off.

Jen has to be the best at everything. Even music, the one thing I have a gift for. It's almost funny because Jen has never had any natural musical talent, but she used to try so hard, just because she wanted to beat me. But she never sang a solo part in the school band. I know it drove her crazy.

Sometimes I like to drive her crazy.

I slurp my ice tea extra loud.

"Darby, stop that. It's disgusting."

"Whatever."

"Do you know what your problem is, Darby? You have no standards. You're uncouth."

"Uncouth? God, you talk like my grandma sometimes. What the hell is your problem, anyway? You're the one who wanted to hang out."

Jen chews on her fingernails for a moment. Even though she considers this a gross habit, she can't help doing it when she's pissed off. Then she folds her hands in her lap and glares at me. "I can't believe that you hooked up with my brother again."

"What do you care? You should be happy for us."

"Because it's always the same with you. You dump him for some other guy. Then you get tired of your new boyfriend because he cheats on you, or doesn't cater to your every wish, and Luke takes you back. You've done it, what ... three times now? Chris, then Jeff, then Matt ... oh, and Gary, how could we forget Gary Weaver, the Big Dick. Am I missing anyone else?"

Jen's criticisms are too close to the truth for me to deny. Especially the Gary thing. I don't know what the hell was going through my primitive brain that night. Yuck.

But I have to say something. I can't let that accusation stand. "Look, Jen, Luke's a big boy. He can make up his own mind."

"You don't get it, do you? He forgives and forgives and forgives, and you don't give a shit about what that costs him."

"Jen, I promise you, I won't hurt your brother. It's going to work out this time." I think I mean it. I hope I mean it. Jen's a human lie detector.

"Fine. Whatever."

She doesn't believe me. She keeps picking at the arms of her lawn chair. She doesn't say it, but I know she thinks Luke's too good for me. Part of me agrees with her.

He's just finished his second year of vet school. I could end up waitressing forever. I can see it now. Luke'll join the vet practice in Turtleford and I'll be working in the bar. Or giving music lessons. Or raising a passel of kids and drowning my disappointment in vodka and prescription drugs like some 1950s housewife.

Luke has soil in his blood. He wants nothing more than to come home and start treating livestock and raising cattle and bison and whatever else he can get his hands on. And I am so hungry for something else, sometimes I can't stand it.

Exactly what I want, I don't know. I'm afraid of the city's concrete, but thrilled by the crowds and the energy. And when I feel restless some nights, I tiptoe to the attic and compose songs on my acoustic guitar, trying to channel Neko Case and Jeff Tweedy and a little bit of myself.

I don't know how to explain this to Luke, though. I think I really love him. But I can't talk to him about it. I don't want to hurt him again.

Fuck it, why am I even thinking about this shit today? I need to chill. I pour a little vodka into my ice tea.

Jen and I flip through newish issues of *People* and *National Enquirer* that Jen's cousins have left behind and talk about nothing. The morning crawls by.

"Billy Bob and Angelina are splitting up." I sip my ice tea as couthly as possible.

"Oh, God, no. After Britney and Justin, I don't think I can take any more," Jen says, totally deadpan.

We snicker and snipe at celebs the rest of the morning.

Finally, at noon, she stands up.

"I need to get going. I told the Wrights I'd go over there to help muck out the barns and exercise the horses."

"Be careful with those crazy horses, Jen. Seriously." For the last few years, Jen's worked for the Wrights every summer, helping with their chuckwagon horses and other work around the farm. This spring, as soon as she finished her exams, she went to outriding school. Much to her mother's distress, she passed her outriding test and is now the only female outrider on the circuit.

Jen's small, maybe five foot three, and she looks vulnerable on those thoroughbreds running full out around the track. But she's athletic and full of grit. If she were a guy, I would say she's got a big set of balls.

"You need a ride home, Darby?"

"No, Luke'll be here in an hour or two."

"Fine." She's chewing on her cheeks, as though she's got more to say, but she turns away abruptly.

"See you later," she chirps over her shoulder, marching through the kitchen and out the door.

Luke arrives at two and fires up the barbeque.

"How are you doing, babe?" he asks, flipping burgers. I hate it when he calls me "babe," but I've never told him.

I consider telling him about our visit with Will this morning. He'd understand, and he could probably help me figure things out. Luke is so good at remembering details and so logical it's almost sickening sometimes. He likes to look at the messiest problems and, as he puts it, "unpack" them. It's like he's doing a jigsaw puzzle — he can shift all the pieces around until they form a picture that makes sense. He'll be a great vet.

But I don't want to turn my uncle into a messy problem for Luke to analyze. In fact, I don't want to talk about my family at all today.

"I'm okay, I guess. Or maybe not. I don't know. I don't want to think about any of it."

"Let's forget about it, then. Want to take the boat out?"

"Yeah, sure."

That evening I fry the walleye while Luke cleans up the loft. We eat on the deck, then head upstairs.

Luke has filled the loft with candles, and Sarah Slean plays on the stereo. He kisses me slowly, runs his hands over my body, then starts undressing me. We shuffle toward the bed, like a couple of junior high kids slow dancing. Still kissing. I lie down, pull Luke on top of me.

It's so hot in the loft. I feel like I might suffocate. And to be honest, the sex has become routine. Luke never switches it up, and I don't have the energy to suggest any changes.

I start thinking about my fight with Jen. Maybe she's right about me and Luke.

Luke suddenly stops, and I know I've been caught daydreaming.

"Is everything all right?" he asks.

"Um, yeah, of course," I say.

"Well, you don't seem into it. Do you want to try something else?"

"I don't know ... me on top?" Maybe if I'm running the show, I'll be a little more focused.

We switch, and my mind starts drifting again. Desperate, I try to rein myself in by concentrating on Luke's eyes. Luke has brown eyes, with gold flecks that spark in the sun. Last week I waited on a guy with the most beautiful black eyes.

Shit. I'm doing it again.

I shut my eyes and lean forward, burying my face in Luke's strong neck. Taste the salt of his skin, feel the grains of sand on his scalp. Try to stay in the moment.

Try not to ask myself if I'm making a big mistake.

# CHAPTER THREE

*The purple clouds are heavy with moisture. When I close my eyes, I can taste rain. It will wash off the dust clinging to the corners of my eyes. It will rush down my body, under my jeans, filling my boots.*

*Sheet lightning flashes. Thunder like a kick drum vibrating. I shiver in the muggy heat. Despite the thunder and lightning, there's not one drop of rain. No breeze disturbs the dust clinging to the grass. I sneeze, and dirty black mucus marks my hand. I wipe it on my jeans.*

*I don't think I've ever been to this place before, but the treeless horizon is familiar. I'm standing on a train track. The rails gleam under the dark sky. So bright, clean, silver.*

*I kneel down, touch the rails. They vibrate slightly. I press my ear to them and hear a high, sing-song vibrato. Each syllable is clear. Des-tin-y, des-tin-y. I jerk my head up, and a low whistle rolls down the tracks.*

*I walk away from the tracks. There's nothing in front of me. No houses break the dark horizon. No roads, no crops, no people, no power lines. Only train tracks, open prairie, and flashing sky. I turn back, watching the tracks. Waiting.*

*The train whistle gradually grows louder. Then, finally, I see the train, a black dot to the northeast. I imagine a headlight, a line of smoke.*

*The vibrato in the tracks grows. I can hear its loud mechanical chant. Des-tin-y, des-tin-y. Faster now. A weak breeze pulls the damp hair around my face, twisting a few strands. It's coming from the train, suddenly closer. Now I can see the light, the train's clean edges. Hear the clang of iron moving against iron. It's moving toward me so fast, I'm suddenly afraid.*

*I'm about to turn away when I see a black mare. It's Magic.*

*Magic is galloping along the track, toward the train. Her gait is so fluid that she looks like she's moving in slow motion. But she flies past me, and I know she's running hard. Her hooves fling pebbles as she passes, and one hits my lower lip. I taste blood.*

*The wind roars now, and Magic flattens her ears to her skull. Her head is sleek as a snake's. I watch her thunder toward the collision point, unable to turn away. The wind and the metal scream of the train fill my ears. I cover my ears, my mouth wide open, screaming.*

I jerk upright, disoriented, sheets soaked in sweat. My alarm clock shrieks at me, and I slam my palm on the snooze. Wipe my sweaty face with the edge of a sheet. Something about the dream is familiar to me. I feel like I've watched the last scene before, but I can't place it.

I think of Magic, and my mom, and my throat tightens up.

My life is a clichéd country song: *My Momma's horse died / And my Momma's gone too / My aunt was murdered this week / And you know I can't lie / I'm not sure if I love you.*

Sorry, Nashville, this hit will have to wait, I think. Gotta go to work today. Even though I'm tired. Even though I feel like all the blood's been drained out of me.

I slide out of bed, dig through the pile of clothes on the floor until I find a denim skirt and a cranberry blouse. They still smell like Bounce, so they must be clean. I pick them up, shuffle to the bathroom, and have a quick shower. Wipe the moisture from the mirror, then wish I hadn't. My skin is ashen and my eyes are red.

I sweep blush onto my cheekbones and chin, and line my eyes with white to counteract the bloodshot look. Pull my hair into a high ponytail and scrub my teeth as I march downstairs and through the living room.

Every time I walk through this canary-yellow room, a small stone shifts at the bottom of my stomach, like a pebble being pushed by the river current. Yellow was Mom's favourite colour. I can still hear her singing off-tune as she slid the yellow roller up and down these walls.

In the kitchen my dad slurps his coffee. I'm surprised he's even here. I stayed up until three in the morning, and he still wasn't home from the cop shop.

Dad's having a bad morning. His eyes are even redder than mine. The table is covered with old issues of *Country Guide*, *Western Producer*, *Maclean's*, *National Geographic*. No breakfast in sight.

"Morning, Darby."

I set my toothbrush on the kitchen counter, swallow the toothpaste froth.

"Morning, Dad."

"Darby? Service'll be Friday next week. Grandpa Kolchak's staying with us, so clean up the spare room. When you have a chance."

"Okay, Dad." Only Dad would give me over a week's notice to clean my CDs and records out of the spare room. He knows me too well.

I wait for a minute, wondering if Dad will say anything else. He picks up the *Producer*, shakes it so the newsprint crackles. I fill my travel mug with bitter coffee, grab an apple, and head to the restaurant. Leave my dad alone with his paper, his coffee, and his ghosts.

About two weeks ago Luke installed a new stereo in my AMC Jeep. He also gave me an MP3 player that I can plug into the stereo with an auxiliary cable. He loaded up the MP3 player with songs, mostly stuff we listened to in high school. Lots of songs from the *Big Shiny Tunes* compilations that MuchMusic used to create. I've left Luke's songs on the player because I don't want to hurt his feelings, but I'm sick of them.

Last night I picked through my CDs and uploaded a bunch of new songs onto the player. Some Tom Waits and Warren Zevon. A large helping of Neko Case, Wilco, The Band, Neil Young, and Joni Mitchell. A dash of Cash, a sprinkle of Sarah Slean, and a pinch of Barenaked Ladies, Chantal Kreviazuk, Ron Sexsmith, and, to top it off, Bowie and Queen "Under Pressure."

By three a.m. I finished, and I listened to my MP3 player until I finally floated into sleep.

I crank up the stereo loud so I can't hear my truck rattling.

I always drive fast when the roads are dry. I like the way my yellow Jeep fishtails on the washboard, almost in slow motion. I'm so used to it I can steer with one hand and hold my coffee in the other, loosening my grip around the handle of the cup when I need to shift up or down.

The first part of my drive to work is straight north. Then I turn onto the 795 grid and follow it as it winds east, then south, then east again. Past the spruce that line the speed curves. Past open alfalfa fields, then east on Dexter Hall road. Past a huge slough that we call Jen's Car Wash because she rolled her car into it. Past Dexter Hall, then through the chunk of Thunderchild Reserve bordering the lake. I always slow down here. Sometimes there are people walking along the side of the road, and I don't want to pelt them with gravel. The road on the reserve narrows a bit and snakes southeast before spitting me out next to the Horseshoe at Horseshoe Bay.

The Horseshoe is a rectangular building, covered with white vinyl siding and sitting at the edge of a dusty gravel parking lot. About two hundred feet from the restaurant is a long, thin strip of white sand and a boat launch. A small store in one half of the building does a brisk business among cabin owners in the summer, selling groceries, ice cream, and gas. The other half is a restaurant, popular with locals year round and packed to the rafters once summer gets rolling. The best part is the wrap-around deck, which overlooks Turtle Lake. It's the perfect place to chomp through a burger and fries before heading back to the beach. One of my earliest memories is of sitting on my mom's lap while she gossiped with Bea and Lena, Jen's mom, on this deck. Mom's voice purring through our bodies, lulling me to sleep.

I started working here part time the summer I turned four-teen. My first paycheque was one hundred seventy-five dollars, plus about seventy-five dollars in tips. I bought two CDs — Ron Sexsmith's self-titled album and *Living Under June* by Jann Ar-den. The rest of my cheque went into my savings account, which I eventually used to buy and fix up my yellow Jeep. A chunk of my pay still goes into the Jeep, for maintenance and gas. I spend a bit on booze and clothes, but I've always tucked a tidy sum into my savings account.

After I flunked out of university, I began working here full time. Now I do the books, order the food and other supplies for the restaurant and store, and schedule the staff. During the summer, I work six days a week, taking only Tuesdays off. I always start at 7:15 to open things up, brew the coffee, mix the batters for pancakes and French toast. The summer staff is made up of high school students without much experience, plus Susan, the current owner. Susan usually drifts in around eight o'clock to take orders while I cook breakfast.

It's 7:10, and already I can tell it'll be a hot day. I jog to the front door, check to see whether it's locked. Of course it is: Susan likes to sleep in. She needs to pay me more, I think as I jiggle my key in the sticky lock. The black horseshoe, hanging right-side-up above the door, vibrates slightly as I struggle with the lock. I throw my shoulder against the door, sending it flying. Trip over something and crash to the floor.

"Fuck!"

My knee is bleeding, and I've spilled coffee on my shirt. I bounce back up, brushing white dust off my legs and arms. Glare at the five-gallon pail that tripped me, then realize that the dingy beige carpet is gone and the faded floral wallpaper has been ripped away. I catch a whiff of coffee wafting from the kitchen. It doesn't smell like our usual Folgers.

In the middle of the dining room there are several cans of paint, a sander, a paintbrush, and a few rollers. Light streams in through the east windows, and I realize the old blinds are gone too. They're impossible to clean, so I should be happy, but everything seems out of place. I feel like I've picked up my guitar to find someone's played it without asking and left it out of tune. I can almost feel the pitch waver through my fingers and up my arms.

As I walk toward the kitchen, a hand reaches out from behind me, grabs my shoulder.

"Aaaahhh!" Instinctively I stomp my foot on the person's instep and simultaneously ram my elbow into ribs. I hear a sharp inhale in my ear and the loose hairs around my neck flutter. As the grip on my shoulder loosens, I whirl around to face my attacker.

A man in frayed jeans and a ratty grey T-shirt stares back at me. He's about five foot ten and slim. Blue eyes and a narrow face with high cheek bones. Brown wavy hair. I start to memorize his face so I can describe it to the cops, then realize he looks familiar. He's been here before.

"Jesus, that hurt," he says. "Where'd you learn that?" He walks toward me, right arm outstretched, left arm clutching his ribs.

"Stay right there!" I step backwards. "Who are you? Where is Susan?"

"Didn't you read the sign on the front door?" I shake my head no. "Well, Susan's moved back to Saskatoon. I'm Jack Cook, and I own the Horseshoe now."

"What? What the hell are you talking about? Wait, don't say anything more. I need more coffee."

"Here, allow me." He refills my mug, hands it back with a nearly charming grin. "We're switching to a new brand, too. I'm a bit of a coffee snob. You like it?" I nod weakly as I take a sip. It's pretty good coffee, I'll give him that.

"And I'm assuming you're Darby? I wasn't expecting you today."

"I always work Wednesdays."

Jack glances at the floor, and I wonder if he's heard about my aunt. "You have a key? Susan didn't mention that."

"Susan sleeps in every day," I snort. "We'd never open on time if she hadn't given me a key. Why'd she sell this place to you, anyway? Or maybe I should ask, why did you buy it?"

"She owed some money, wanted out. I owed her a favour."

"Must be some favour, buying a place like this. You'll have to work your ass off to make any money here. Don't get any ideas about raising prices, either, especially for the coffee."

Jack fills his own cup with coffee, adds about six teaspoons of sugar. And suddenly I remember who he is. He used to come in here all the time with Susan, years before she bought this place. She always got after him for adding so much sugar to his coffee and for tipping too much.

"How long have you worked here, Darby?"

"Seven years."

He looks surprised. "How old are you?"

"Twenty-one. Look, I don't understand what's going on here.

I take a couple extra days off, and suddenly everything's changed and Susan's disappeared into thin air. And you're here. Who are you, exactly? And why did Susan up and leave?"

"I'm Susan's ex-husband. Susan was in the middle of a crisis. I felt bad, so I helped her out."

Gambling or drinking, I'd bet. Maybe both. "Why do you care? I mean, you're divorced."

"The divorce was my fault. But I never wanted it."

"Oh." All this change. People leaving, the place torn apart with no warning. My hands are shaking. Maybe it's the caffeine.

"Darby? You're going to college this fall?" Jack is still rubbing his ribs with his left hand, holding his coffee with his right.

"Yeah. Music program at MacEwan College in Edmonton."

"Listen, I need help. Learning how to manage staff, how to do inventory. Susan said you managed the inventory and helped with the books. Could you do that for me?"

"Sure, I guess. Susan paid me ten bucks an hour, so ..."

"How does twenty sound?"

"Uh, great!"

Jack smiles, puts down his coffee, extends his hand. I take it, hoping he doesn't notice the shaking. But his smile fades a little, and I know he has.

# CHAPTER FOUR

We hold Bea's funeral in Turtleford, in the lobby of the hockey rink, which doubles as a community hall.

On the day of the funeral, Dad and I go into Turtleford early. I've agreed to play "Helpless" on the piano, and I need to run through it a few times. I might sing it too, if I'm up to it.

Bea always loved Neil Young, and I performed this song for her fortieth birthday party. That night she wore a chunky turquoise necklace Uncle Will had given her, her dark hair pinned up, a little messy. Bea and Mom stood together, Bea's skinny arm around Mom's soft waist, both swaying a little as I sang at her out-of-tune bench piano. When I finished, Will presented her with a bouquet of forty white roses, and she started to cry. She asked me to help her arrange them in vases. When we were alone in the kitchen, she slipped me one rose.

"I can't take it, Aunty," I said. "It's your rose."

"Will got it wrong, sweetie. I'm thirty-nine and holding." She winked and pulled me into a hug. "Besides, you're like my own daughter, and I'm proud of you."

I blink, clearing the clouds from my eyes, then sit down at the piano. I'm nervous even though the hall's empty right now. I practise for about half an hour, and then Dad and I go for coffee.

At one o'clock Dad and I walk into the packed hall. Most of the chairs are taken, and people have clustered around the doors. The crowd parts for us, moving like water. There are people here I don't know. Lots of them. Women in dark boot-leg jeans, tailored blouses, and pointy heels, big sunglasses hiding eyes. Men in sport coats and ties, one of them subtly checking his PDA before realizing that he has no service. I want to smash his gadget, break the women's sunglasses. Drive the strangers out of the lobby like rats from a grain elevator.

I am surprised at, and a little ashamed of, my possessiveness of Bea. Her world was bigger than this little town, this rural slice of northwest Saskatchewan. Her scrapbooks were filled with mementos from places she visited. Photos and sketches of urban landscapes, reviews of her shows. Edmonton, Saskatoon, Regina, Calgary, Winnipeg, Vancouver, Montreal, Halifax. I used to flip through those books and daydream about singing in those cities, a big band behind me. And now I'm at her funeral, resenting these outsiders for caring about her.

And maybe resenting her for not taking me to those shows. Not introducing me to that part of her world. She always said she was going to take me, but for some reason it never worked out.

Pauline Brooks, Bea's agent from Saskatoon, is a few rows from the front. She's sitting with her husband, Harvey. Pauline's normally plump face is impossibly swollen, and her eyes are puffy and red. I haven't seen Pauline in three years, not since Bea's exhibit at the Mendel, and her hair is pure white now. Pauline and Bea went to art school together, so I know they're roughly the same age, but Pauline suddenly looks much older.

I wonder if something happened to Pauline. If she's been ill. Bea never said anything.

Pauline meets my eyes, mouths *I'm so sorry*. Then leans into her husband, sobbing.

I walk on.

Luke and Jen are near the front, right beside the aisle. As I walk by, Luke touches my hand. The heat is suffocating, and as I sit down next to Uncle Will, I can already feel myself wilting.

Grandpa Kolchak walks up, still tall and straight as a lodge-pole pine. The young usher holding Grandpa's arm gestures to the empty seat in our row, beside Will, but Grandpa shakes him off, a little roughly. He turns and sits two rows behind us. I turn around, try to send him a smile, but he's glaring at the floor.

This is going to be a long service.

Grandpa Kolchak wanted to hold a family service at the Conglomerate Cliffs, south of Maple Creek, later this summer, and scatter Bea's ashes from the cliffs. It's what she'd want, he told us. I think he's right, but Will wouldn't go for it.

"She's not from Maple Creek anymore, Ivan. She belongs at our ranch," Will said yesterday afternoon when Grandpa brought it up. Grandpa told Will to go to hell, and I thought he was going to take a swing at Will, but Grandpa Swank pulled him into the verandah, and then they went to the barn and had a couple beers. Dad told Will, "He's just upset, Will," and I was feeling upset myself, so I went to the attic and dug through Mom and Dad's old records until I came up with Joni Mitchell's *Blue*. I stretched out on the floor, closed my eyes, and listened to the whole thing once through before I went back downstairs.

The stage at the front is an exhibit of Bea's work, almost enough to distract everyone from the simple black urn. A few watercolours, acrylics, mixed media. Blown-up photos of her last piece, an installation at Brightsand Lake. Dozens of tea lights glued to wide chunks of driftwood, floating in the dark water. Shards of mirror glued back to back on fishing line connecting the driftwood, reflecting the light. Like a spider web made of stars. I'd helped her set the driftwood in the water, carefully lit the candles. The lake was still that night, and the only ripples were from our canoe paddles. As we drifted along the edge of the spider web, Bea took pictures, and I started writing a song in my head.

*We float at the edge of night, shut out from the web of stars. The dark sky reflects our pain. I wish I could start all over again.*

George Henderson, the Anglican minister from the nearby village of Mervin, takes his place behind the podium and begins reading from the Book of Common Prayer. The burial of the dead. I am the resurrection and the life, all that stuff.

Bea never seemed overly religious, but she went to church in Mervin sometimes. She said George knew how to deliver a good sermon. She said he knew how to find wisdom in the Bible, something not everyone could do. She said he was insightful.

Will used to tease her about her occasional solo trips to church. "You just go to flirt with George Henderson," he'd say, smiling.

"You know I only have eyes for you, darling," she'd reply with the faintest smile.

Uncle Will's idea of church was fishing. He'd go to Turtle Lake every Sunday he could. In the winter, people gathered in his ice shack, which grew larger over the years. Two years ago he converted an old camper into a fishing shack, and he'd hold court in there every Sunday as friends and neighbours stopped in for a drink (or a few) while skidooing. Will kept it well stocked with rye and beer, and even had a thermos of coffee for the very few teetotalers. "No one leaves my shack thirsty," he'd say.

Bea wasn't much for ice fishing, but she'd often fish with him in June. Will didn't drink much on those spring trips. They'd usually come back with their limit of jacks, and often some walleye too.

I went with Will sometimes too, but I didn't really have the patience for fishing. Neither did Luke. But Uncle Will taught Jen and Sam all his tricks. He said either of them could be fishing guides if they wanted. Will even had a friend with a fishing camp up north of La Ronge, and Sam started working for him after high school.

George's voice catches, and the stumble pulls me back into the present. The service. He's reciting a psalm now. The one that talks about God being a refuge and turning man to destruction, and children of men, and all that.

"As soon as Thou scatterest them they are even as a sleep; and fade away suddenly like the grass. In the morning it is green, and groweth up; but in the evening it is cut down, dried up, and withered." George's voice is steady again, rhythmic as waves lapping the dock.

Are we this vulnerable, that we can wither as easily as grass in a drought? Are our lives so brief and insignificant in God's eyes that he looks at us the way we look at a patch of lawn? So temporary?

I'm not sure I'm getting the right message here. I tune out of the sermon again, glance around the room.

Karin Polley, the rookie cop, is here with Cardinal and Steele. They're all to my right, their backs against one of the large windows overlooking the indoor hockey rink. None of them is in uniform, but they're obviously studying the crowd. They're not even looking at the minister.

One of the acrylics at the front of the room is a landscape of poplars in the winter. The bare branches are silhouettes against the sky. It's these fragments of grey-blue in between dark branches that really catch the eye. Darkness and light. Negative space.

Negative space is all around us. Bea explained it as the space around a subject, or between solid forms. Imagine Bugs Bunny running through a door and leaving a rabbit-shaped hole behind. The door around the hole is the negative space. That's how Betty Edwards explained it in her book, *Drawing on the Right Side of the Brain*.

Negative space is more than emptiness. It's also the pause between each note I sing. It's the words I think but never speak.

It gives structure to a piece of music, texture to a relationship, form to a subject. Without negative space we would never be able to see an individual tree in the forest.

Bea's body is gone and she's left negative space. Just like Bugs leaving his silhouette in the door.

The cops are trying to reconstruct the space around Bea. They can't see her clearly right now, but if they can see the world around her, they might be able to make out her form. They need to find out what people will say and won't say about her. They need to know her habits (coffee and scrambled eggs every morning) and know what she avoided (gory movies and TV shows like *CSI* and *Law & Order* — she said they gave her nightmares). Once the cops know all this, they'll know what doesn't fit. Then they might know who killed Bea.

Yesterday Jack and I were painting the dining room of the Horseshoe when Sergeant Cardinal strolled through the door.

"We're not open," Jack hollered.

"Yeah, I can see that," said Cardinal. "I'm here to talk to Darby."

I put down my roller, wiped the green paint from my hands onto my cut-off shorts, and followed Cardinal outside.

"Darby, as you know, we pulled your aunt's car out of Turtle River."

"No, I didn't know, actually."

"I assumed your dad told you."

"No one tells me anything around here." I lit a smoke.

They'd found Bea's Impala just off the reserve road, on the way to Turtleford. They weren't sure exactly what happened, but she'd been driving very fast, at least 120 kilometres an hour (assuming it was her driving), when the car left the road. They'd checked to see if the car had been rammed from behind, but it hadn't. But that didn't mean someone wasn't chasing her, Cardinal said.

After they'd pulled it out and popped the trunk, they found

a large suitcase packed with clothes, her photo albums, cameras, and sketch books, and fifteen thousand dollars cash.

"We've been through Will and Bea's bank accounts, and there haven't been any unaccounted-for withdrawals over the last year that would add up to anything close to that sum. Do you know where she would have got the cash?" Cardinal pulled a notepad and pen from his shirt pocket.

"No. I have no idea. Maybe she sold a few colts?"

"The money from all those sales is accounted for. She deposited all of it in the farm account."

"Did you ask her agent? Maybe from her art sales."

"No, the money from all her sales is accounted for, too."

"I really have no idea, then."

"Would anyone lend her that kind of money?"

I looked at Cardinal skeptically. "I don't know anyone around here with an extra fifteen grand in cash."

"But if anyone was going to lend her any money, who would it be?"

"I don't know ... maybe Lena Cherville. But I don't think the Chervilles have the cash, not with two kids in university."

"Okay, now the last time you saw her, you thought she was going somewhere. Where do you think she'd go?"

"I really don't know." I thought for a moment. "She was going south, right? I mean, if she was going west, toward Lloyd, she'd go through Walburg. So if she was heading toward Turtleford, she was going south. Maybe to Saskatoon or even further south, right? But she didn't say anything to me, and I didn't notice anything. And I don't know where she'd be going, except maybe to see her agent."

They'd checked with Pauline Brooks already, and she wasn't expecting Bea, Cardinal said.

"Did anything seem out of the ordinary that day you saw her?" Cardinal asked.

"Well, nothing other than she seemed happier than normal.

But kind of tense, too. I don't know. I already told the other cop — I mean police officer — about that."

"Anything else? Anything seem out of place, even since she died?"

"No ..." I hesitated, thinking about the bleach smell when Jen and I visited Will. I didn't want to turn the cops against Will, though, instead of looking for the real killer.

"Are you sure? Anything might help, no matter how insignificant."

"No, I can't think of anything I haven't already told you."

Cardinal sighed. "Darby, we're trying to help your family, but we need your help. And we can't help you if you withhold information."

"Jesus Christ, I'm not withholding anything!"

"Okay, fine, Darby. Was Bea left-handed?"

"Yes ... but she could paint with both hands. I think she could even write with her right hand. Why?"

"The autopsy showed that her left wrist had been fractured several times in the past. Do you remember how she was injured?"

"Yeah, I already told Steele. She had a few wrecks breaking colts."

"When was the last one?"

"Maybe a couple years ago. I'm not sure."

"And do you know why it would always be her left wrist?"

"I don't know. Maybe she always broke her fall with that hand."

"Did you see any of the accidents?"

"No."

"Did anyone see them?"

"I don't know. Maybe my Dad or Will? Sometimes we helped her, but she worked alone a lot."

"Anything else you noticed? Things you thought were minor. Bruises, even."

"No, I didn't notice anything like that. She always had

migraines, though. The pain made her throw up."

Cardinal asked me an exhausting series of questions about Bea's migraines — what triggered them, their duration, their frequency. I told him they always came after she'd been painting frantically for several days and not eating or sleeping much. I told him they seemed to come more frequently in the last two years. He scribbled madly in his little notebook.

"Okay. Thank you, Darby. Call us if anything else comes to mind." Cardinal tucked his notepad back in his pocket.

"Wait, wait. Can you tell me how she died? Please? I want to know."

Cardinal hesitated, like he wasn't sure how to tell me. "I guess I can tell you. The autopsy confirmed that she was strangled."

I digested this for a moment. How long would it have been before she lost consciousness? How much did she suffer? My hands were shaking again, and I didn't want Cardinal to notice. I dropped my smoke, put my hands in my pockets.

I didn't want to ask the next question, but I had to know. I couldn't stand not knowing what happened to her. All of her.

"Did you find her finger? It bugs me, you know, that her finger was, um, missing."

"How did you know about that?" Cardinal's tone was curt. I wished I hadn't asked.

"I saw her hand ... when I found her."

"Darby, does anyone else know? Did you tell anyone about this?"

"No. Why would I tell anyone something like that?"

"Did Luke notice?"

"No. He would have told me. Why does it matter?"

Cardinal inhaled, puffed his cheeks up like a squirrel before blowing out the air.

"Because the only people who know are us and the killer. Darby, did Bea wear a wedding band?" Cardinal pulled out his notebook.

"Yeah, always. Her joints were swollen, so she couldn't take it off without soap. Was she still alive when her finger was, you know..."

"No. Post-mortem." Cardinal flicked his wrist, flipping the notepad shut. "Do not tell anyone about this. Do you understand? Not a soul."

"I won't. I wish I could forget it."

"Listen, Darby, I am sorry about your aunt. She didn't deserve this. We're on her side, you know."

"Yeah."

As I sit through the funeral service, something tries to surface in the dark waters of my mind. Something that will fill in a bit of the space around Bea. I can't quite make it out, and the harder I try, the muddier it becomes. I give up, and it slips back under the surface.

I try to read the faces around me without being too obvious. But the only people I can see well without craning my neck are my family. Dad, Grandma and Grandpa Swank, Will, their faces all dark with grief. The shadows under Will's eyes are dark blue. They look bruised. And he has a bandage on his jaw, probably a nick from shaving. But overall he looks a lot better than he did a few days ago. His colour is back, anyway. He notices me studying him. Unable to meet my eye, he goes back to staring at the floor.

"And now, Bea's niece, Darby Swank, will perform a song."

I stand, smooth my red skirt, walk to the piano. Pause, trying to decide whether to sing or just play the piano. Will I hold it together?

I can sing this for Aunt Bea, I decide, and begin.

If my voice were an animal, it would be a prairie bison bull. Big and strong, with lots of stamina. I struggle to control it sometimes, to make it turn quickly enough to nail the next note. But today it's a perfectly tuned instrument, and I pour all my grief into the song. When I finish, Grandma Swank looks up and nods solemnly at me.

Dad stands up to deliver the eulogy. Dad is so steady, so reined in, that I can hardly stand it. When I was a little kid, if I hurt myself, Dad would pull me to my feet, assure me that I was okay, and tell me to get back on the horse. Usually I would stop crying and climb back on my Shetland pony, or bike, or whatever I'd fallen from. There was no point in demanding sympathy from Dad unless I had broken bones.

It was the same after Mom died. He could take over the cooking and help with my homework, but he couldn't talk about how sad he was. He hardly even talked about Mom most of the time. Every now and then, he would spit out a single story, like about the time Mom's rhubarb–apple pie took first place at the Turtleford fair and she crowed about it for a month. (Grandma Swank took second, and she scowled every time she saw Mom for two months.) But once he finished a story, he'd never retell it. It was as though a piece of my mom disappeared forever every time he finished a story.

Bea would have me over for coffee and show me old photos and tell me stories about Mom, too. She'd take her time telling them, and tell them over and over. Like how every time Mom won a barrel race on Magic, she'd celebrate afterwards by getting cowboys to buy her Scotch on ice. (I'd wondered why my uncles called her Scotty at family reunions.) Or how she eventually taught all the younger kids, boys and girls, to pack their own lunches, wash their own laundry, and even take turns cooking meals. "She was the most impatient, short-tempered teacher we ever saw, so we learned real quick," Bea always said.

"And when your two uncles got married, May told their new wives that those boys could cook as well as, or even better than, most women. And they could, and they did." Bea laughed. "The boys didn't appreciate her sharing that information at first."

Even after I'd heard everything and seen all the photos, I still needed to remember her.

Dad clears his throat and begins to speak. "I'll never forget Bea's wedding, in the meadow where she and Will Fletcher would make their home. I was Will's best man, and we stood together, waiting for the bride to walk down the aisle. A black horse ran out of the trees toward the guests. Perched on top of that horse, riding sidesaddle, was Bea. Her veil trailed behind her like a victory flag, and she looked as triumphant as a general."

I can't take it. I push through the crowd, through the dark, humid lobby, toward the open doors. I emerge into the bright sunshine, gulp air as though I've been underwater.

Luke follows me outside. He pulls me into a tight hug and drops several small kisses on the top of my head. I breathe in the fresh-cut-grass smell of his cologne and cry.

Once I'm done crying, Luke and I head to the Turtle River Café, a small coffee and sandwich shop on Main Street. It used to be a photography studio, full of fake Greek pillars and backdrops and other props. Luke had his graduation photos taken here. I was his grad escort, so I was in several of them. Two years later, Jen, Sam, and I were here having our own grad photos taken. Small-town rituals.

I wonder what happened to all the props. I imagine them in some old barn or storage shed, layered with dust and cobwebs.

We sit at a maple table at the back of the restaurant, drinking coffee and waiting for the rest of my family to arrive. The front of the restaurant is all windows, making it easy to watch people walking down Main Street. People going into the pharmacy next door. A middle-aged lady primping her hair as she walks by. She must have been in the hair salon down the street.

Sam's parents go into the Credit Union across the street. I thought they'd be at the funeral. They've lived down the road from us since the early '80s, when they moved out here as a late part of the "back to the land" wave.

I watch for twenty minutes, but they don't emerge. I wonder if they're refinancing their mortgage or something. Maybe they're having money problems — why else would they miss Bea's funeral? Sam's mom is a teacher and his dad works in the oil patch, so they should be okay for money, but who knows.

This is how rumours get started, I think. Snoopy people sitting in the coffee shop on Main Street.

After half an hour, my dad and Grandpa Kolchak walk through the door. Grandpa walks right up to me and wraps me in a bear hug.

"Good job, Darbs," he says.

"Thanks, Grandpa. Ummm, you're squeezing me a bit hard."

"Sorry." He releases me, looks at Luke. "And who is this young man?"

"Uh, Grandpa, this is Luke. You met him at my grad."

"Good to see you again, Luke. I assume you're treating my granddaughter well?"

"Yes, sir. Quite a handshake you have there, sir."

"You bet it is." Grandpa smiles, gives Luke's hand one last squeeze, then heads for the coffee.

"Your grandpa's quite the guy, Darby."

"Yeah. Mom said when she was a teenager, he used to scare off all her boyfriends. He's actually pretty mellow now."

There are about thirty people in the restaurant. Just family and close friends, mostly, standing and talking as they sip coffee and eat Nanaimo bars. I don't feel like talking to anyone, so Luke and I sit in the corner, avoiding eye contact. Despite my antisocial behaviour, a big lady with long white hair spots me and shuffles toward me. Will's mom. Great Aunt Jessie.

"Shit," I whisper "Tell her I have to go to the bathroom."

"Sit down," says Luke, pulling me down. "You're going to have to take this one for the team."

"Soooo sorry about Bea," Jessie coos as she grasps my hand, squeezing tightly. "She was such a lovely woman, so kind-hearted ..." She reaches for my cheeks, stops herself before she pinches them. Thank God.

I nod solemnly, trying to peek around her without being too rude as she prattles on. There's a ruckus by the door, but I can't see around Jessie's round frame. I stand up, but Jessie is tall enough to block the scene. Whatever's going on, my grandpa's at the centre of it. I can hear his voice above the quiet conversation.

Jessie realizes the action is behind her and steps aside as she turns around. Now I see my seventy-eight-year-old grandfather shove Uncle Will, sending him staggering backwards into the dessert table. The table tilts, and trays of squares slide to the ground, landing with a crash that silences everyone in the room. Will steadies himself, and for a second I think he's going to lunge at Grandpa Kolchak. Then he inhales visibly and steps back.

"Helluva way to express your condolences, Ivan," Will snipes.

Grandpa is breathing hard, his eyes wild. Everyone has formed a horseshoe around him and Will, so that they are penned in on three sides by people and by the windows on the other side. We stare, mouths gaping. A few people look excited, like hockey fans about to see a fight.

My family is so awesome.

"Well, what do you have to say for yourself, old man?" Will sneers.

Grandpa looks up at me, and suddenly all the fight leaves his body. He shrinks. He opens the door and slams it behind him. The little silver bells above the door shake violently.

I realize this is the only chance I'll get to talk to Grandpa. I rush after him, catching him just as he's getting into his old Ford Taurus.

"Grandpa ... what the hell?"

"I'm sorry, Darby," he says, staring at the steering wheel. "I don't know what I was thinking. I'm just a stupid old man."

"Grandpa ... no, you're not. I don't know what you are, but you're not stupid, anyway," I say awkwardly.

"You sound just like your grandma." He smiles. Then he reaches into the backseat, rummaging through a mess of empty grocery bags and loose paper. "I brought this for you. Just about forgot to give it to you."

It's a red shoebox. Grandpa has scrawled "May" across the top.

"Thanks, Grandpa."

Grandpa Kolchak gets out of his car, gives me a long, hard hug. "I love you, Darby," he says, his voice thick and muddy. I've never heard Grandpa say he loves anyone, except when he visited my mom in the hospital just before she died.

"I love you too, Grandpa. You don't have to go."

"Oh, I don't think I'm welcome back in there. Take care of yourself, darling."

"I will, Grandpa."

Luke drives me home around suppertime. He wants me to stay with him at the cabin tonight, but I want to be alone. Dad's not around when I get home, so I reheat some lasagna, wash it down with a can of Great Western Light, and head to my room.

When I was a little girl, Mom used to make up stories for me while she tucked me into bed. They always started with "Once upon a time," and ended with "They lived happily ever after." In between someone would have to fight an ogre, break a curse, solve a riddle, or find a magic key.

At the end of every story, she'd tell me not to share it with anyone, that it was our secret. I liked having parts of her to myself, even if they were only silly stories. I never told them to anyone, even after she died. This box of stuff is like one last secret that we can share.

I sit cross-legged on my bed as I open the box and go carefully through the contents. Inside are several old pictures of Mom, most from when she was a little girl. Mom and Bea riding their Shetland pony, Babe. Mom bottle-feeding a Hereford calf. A couple of Mom as a teenager, and one of Mom in an orange polyester bridesmaid dress at Bea's wedding.

At the very bottom of the box is a slim envelope. The address reads "Bea Kolchak, Maple Creek, SK S0N 1N0."

The paper inside is crammed with Mom's precise, small writing. No margins on the side. Just looking at the crowded page makes me anxious.

*Dear Bea,*
*Thanks for sending the sketches from our wedding. I can't believe how detailed your memory is sometimes. It's hard to understand how you almost flunked out of grade nine, but I guess I should let that go since you finally got through high school.*

God, my mom was a hard-ass from way back, wasn't she?

*I know you're off to Calgary for art school soon, but I'd like to set you up with Will before you go. He hasn't stopped talking about you since our wedding. Wouldn't it be lovely if you two hit it off? Will's like a brother to Roy, you know. Technically, they're cousins, but Will spent every summer, and lots of holidays, with Roy. Those boys had no blood brothers, only sisters, and Will's dad was such a drunk, they really are best friends.*

*I don't know how Will turned out so well. He's so hard-working and has such business sense (more than my own husband, unfortunately). And, as you already know, he's the life of every dance. All jokes and charm and light feet. Jolene, Roy's mom, likes to take credit for raising him, but that woman is so hard, I can't see how either of the boys kept their warmth. Jessie is much kinder, but her head's full of feathers. I think Will takes after Roy's dad, Rob, the most, even though they're not blood.*

*I guess it goes to show a man doesn't have to inherit the sins of the father.*

*You should come up for a visit this summer, before you head back to Calgary. But don't mention my little plan to Roy. He thinks you're too young. It's not like I'm telling you to marry Will, at least not right away. Anyway, you're not that young, are you? You're just about done at SAIT. If you're really going to be a poor artist, you should think about finding a husband who can support you.*

*xoxo*
*Your Big Sister,*
*May*

I always thought my mom became toxic after she had me, as though it were somehow my fault. Obviously she had been practising for a long time before I came along. I taste bile in the back of my throat. I put down the letter, exhale slowly.

There's a reason Mom was so controlling. She had to run the household from the age of eleven on. She didn't get to finish her childhood, or finished it too early, depending which way you want to look at it. I never really appreciated how hard it must have been for my mom, the oldest of four children, until she died. Grandpa Kolchak was there, but in some ways he wasn't. He had lost his taste for life, Mom told me once.

"He had no joy, at least not until you were born. The first grandchild."

"How did he go on?" I'd asked.

She paused for a moment, looked at me with her eyebrows raised. As though it were a strange question. Then, maybe remembering whatever Bea had told her, she lowered her eyebrows.

"He went on because he had to. We all did. For each other."

I put the letter back in the envelope and stand in front of the mirror. Mom always said I looked more like Bea's daughter than her own. Aunt Bea and I have the same long face, beanpole frame, and wavy black hair. But I have my mom's full lips and my dad's grey eyes and fair skin. Mom's big gestures and Dad's music.

I think of Will's father and remember how haunted Will looked when Jen and I visited him a few days ago.

Mom was wrong, I think to myself. We always carry our families with us. Even if we try to forget them, they can pop up when we least expect it.

# CHAPTER FIVE

Jack and I decide to re-open the Horseshoe at five o'clock on June 12. We prepare a special mid-week smorg as a celebration. At four thirty, there's a knock on the screen door. I hurry to the front and find Jen and Sam waiting outside.

Jen and Sam are one of those weird opposites-attract couples that somehow worked through high school, but seem destined to crumble. Sam, like many of the kids in this neighbourhood (known locally as "the bush"), is the product of two back-to-the-landers. He's laid back to the extreme. He guides American hunters in the fall and lives with Jen the rest of the time, working odd jobs. He's the only person who dares tell Jen to relax.

They seem like they're good for each other, but in the last year Jen's been tense and restless. She picks at Sam constantly for things like drinking and driving and his lack of ambition. They rarely smile when they're together now.

Jen is starting to realize that while Sam was good enough for high school, he's not going to cut it in her adult life. He's a nice guy, but a little lazy and irresponsible. He's still like a sixteen-year-old boy, and he doesn't have much incentive to grow up.

I still love him like a brother, though, even with all his flaws. Or maybe partly because of his flaws. I don't know.

Sam grins at me, his fist poised to knock again.

"Hey, Littlefoot, let us in," he says. A nickname that began in our childhood, taken from *The Land Before Time*, the tale of baby dinosaurs on a quest. Sam's the only one who still calls me that. He thinks my size-ten feet are hilarious.

I let them in. "It'll be a few minutes before the coffee's ready," I say.

They smile and nod, in no hurry for coffee, and I duck into the kitchen to see how the smorg is coming. Jack is checking the ham and Becky, a local high-school girl, is chopping lettuce for the salad. Jack spots me and gives me two thumbs up.

By five thirty, the Shoe is full up, with two groups waiting near the front door for a table to clear. Becky zips from table to table, quick as a honeybee, a coffeepot in one hand and dirty dishes in the other. Busy as she is, she also gives each table a sweet dose of gossip.

I notice people pretending not to look at me, and I know they're talking about Bea's murder. I feel like a gorilla at the zoo, trying to ignore the gawking tourists. Fucking Becky. Who knows what she's saying about Bea? Too bad she's such a good worker — I can't ask Jack to fire her.

Soon I don't have much time to think about Becky. More and more people are waiting at the door, and the food is going fast. I run between the kitchen and the buffet table, hauling out more scalloped potatoes, more Caesar, pasta, and garden salads, steamed asparagus, slices of honey-glazed ham, apple and lemon meringue pies. A few people are walking toward the till, bills in hand. I wipe my hands on my blue apron and rush over to ring them through. Smile, joke with customers, be sure to thank those who drop change, clinking, into the wide-mouth Mason jar that holds our tips.

Don and Betty Manning walk up. They've been coming here for years, and I don't think they've tipped so much as fifty cents in that time. I used to be nice to Don, even when he hit on me while his wife stared at her plate. I don't bother anymore. In fact, I'm a little hostile. I mean, what kind of middle-aged man hits on young women in front of his wife? And what kind of woman takes that shit? Even Becky doesn't banter with them like she does with every other customer.

"Still not filling out, are you, honey?" He's leering at my chest.

"Well, you sure are," I reply, patting my belly. He scowls as I hand him his change.

Jen and Sam are waiting behind them. They're both grinning at my insult.

"You guys taking off?"

"Yeah, I have to go riding tonight," Jen says. "Hey, Darby, did Susan really lose the restaurant to Jack in a card game?"

"Oh, I don't think so. Sixteen, total. Or eight each." Jen pulls out her wallet, gives me a twenty and waves away her change. I drop the toonies in the tip jar, listen to the hollow clink.

"And is Jack really a drug dealer?" Sam asks.

"Sam! Don't listen to Becky! She says everyone's a drug dealer," I laugh.

"Well, Darby, sometimes she's right," Jen retorts.

"Rarely. Anyway, no, he's not."

"Too bad," Sam whispers. "We could use better-quality pot around here." Jen elbows him in the ribs, then looks around to make sure no one heard him.

"Okay, see you guys later."

"You bet." Jen gives me a wide smile as they leave, and I think maybe everything's cool between us.

Despite the air conditioning in the restaurant, the kitchen is hell. As I put together more salad, I can feel sweat streaming along the sides of my nose, dripping down my legs, and collecting in my sneakers. The mad rush is tapering off now, so I pour myself a glass of cold water, remove my apron, and head out the back door for a quick smoke break. I take my first drag, and Jack finds me.

"Was everything okay?" he asks. "Did they like the food?"

"Sure, they liked it," I say. "Everyone loves a smorg."

"Good. How about the coffee? Did they like the coffee?"

"Oh, yeah, everyone liked the coffee. We did good, Jack. They'll be back tomorrow."

Jack's face relaxes into a smile. "Can I bum a smoke?"

Just as we finish our cigarettes, Becky crashes through the screen door, yelling.

"Darby! Jack!"

"Jesus, what is it, Becky?" Jack sounds exasperated. He's just finished telling me that Becky's gossiping bugs him, but he doesn't know how to bring it up with her.

"There's a fire!"

"A fire! Where?" I run into the kitchen, trying to locate the flames while reaching for the fire extinguisher. Thank God Jack had the sense to install one in the kitchen.

"No, not here! Across the road." She pulls me out the front door. I stare, slack-jawed, at the thick column of smoke spiralling into the sky. "What should we do?" I look at the fire extinguisher I'm still holding and laugh.

"Call the fire department," I say. Becky runs inside, searching for the cordless phone.

I sink to the ground and watch the mountain of smoke grow wider. As the fire spreads, it pushes up more and more smoke. Soon it will block out the sun, I think, and we'll never see the sky again.

I'm standing with the last of the customers outside the front door, watching the fire, when we hear a roar and turn, amazed, as a water bomber skims the lake, collecting a payload to drop on the fire.

"Jack! Check this out!"

Jack comes running out just as the water bomber lifts into the sky.

Just then Karin Polley, the new Turtleford cop, pulls into the parking lot and strides toward us. "Listen, you're going to have to shut down immediately," she says. "We're evacuating this whole beach. It looks like the fire is going to jump the road."

Jack's face goes white, but he doesn't argue. We begin clearing everyone out, not even ringing the last few customers through the till. Most leave cash on the tables.

"Darby, can you and Becky finish up in here?" Jack asks. "I need to take care of some stuff outside."

Half an hour later I send Becky home and go outside where I find Jack on a ladder, cleaning old leaves out of the gutters. Considering the volcano of smoke and flame across the road, it seems futile.

"You should probably get going," I say.

"I don't have insurance. Susan let it lapse, and I didn't get around to renewing it." He climbs down the ladder and starts hooking up the garden hose.

"Oh. Shit."

Across the gravel road, the fire licks up mature black spruce and dry underbrush. A hot wind gusts in our direction and embers soar toward us like red-hot beetles, landing in the tall, dry grass on the west side of the Shoe. Jack quickly shoots water into the grass, smothering the embers.

"I'm going to get this roof as wet as possible before the cops come back," Jack says. "This is a lot to ask, but before you go, could you knock down that grass?"

I pull the weed eater out of the shed beside the kitchen and cut all the surrounding tufts of grass down to bare dirt. Then I rake up all the grass, put it in a garbage bag, and throw the bag in the back of my truck. I finish just as Jack unhooks the garden hose. The shingles are dripping wet.

"I don't know how long that'll work, but at least I gave it a try," he says. "We should probably get out of here."

It looks like the fire has already crossed the road south of us, so we take the road through the reserve, then turn west. Jack follows me in his green Honda CRV. I drive fast — one twenty, one thirty — my nearly empty truck bed fish-tailing across the washboard. When I reach Jen and Luke's parents' farm, I hit the brakes. Down the half-mile driveway, I can see an inferno of smoke and flame. If it hasn't reached their yard, it's very close.

I turn down the driveway, and Jack follows me. I drive slowly now, not wanting to get trapped on this narrow lane surrounded by tinderbox forest. As we get closer, the smoke seeps into the truck more and more, like water. I roll up my windows and close my vents, but it doesn't help.

Once I reach the yard, I notice there are already several trucks and cars, though not many people visible. They must all be in the bush, fighting the fire. Beside the house Sam and Luke are in the one-ton, with a full water tank on the back. They see me pull up and wave at me to follow. I see Sam mouth *Littlefoot*.

Jack parks his SUV and jumps in beside me.

"Where are we?" he asks.

"Lena and Ross Cherville's farm," I say.

The one-ton trundles down a narrow road leading southeast of the farmyard. We follow slowly. Now I can feel the heat on my face and in my throat. I wish I'd brought a bottle of water. Finally we reach a small clearing. People emerge from the surrounding bush, holding shovels and five-gallon pails. Their faces are dirty, making their eyes seem whiter and larger. The smoke is so thick here I can't see more than ten feet into the trees. The one-ton jerks to a stop, and Luke and Sam leap out of the cab. Already people are filling up five-gallon pails, passing them down the line. I see Jen emerge from the bush. I grab a five-gallon pail of water and follow Jen back into the dry muskeg.

The smoke is disorienting, and once I find myself heading closer to the heart of the fire when I want to go for a refill of water. Lena Cherville shows up shortly after we get there and takes over as water truck driver, caterer, and a million other tasks. When she brings us ham and cheese sandwiches, I gulp down my bread like a dog. As more people arrive, I trade in my five-gallon pail for a shovel, hoping it will be easier than hauling water over the deadfall.

Smoke makes the evening grow dark more quickly than normal. As night falls, the moon rises, fat and bloody. I gaze up in awe for a moment, then continue throwing dirt on smouldering embers. The ash and dirt mixes with my sweat. I glance at Luke, shovelling beside me, and he winks. I start singing "We Are the Champions," the Queen classic that we always used to sing while playing floor hockey. Any time anyone scored a goal, the whole team would burst out singing "We Are the Champions." Luke joins in, almost yelling he's singing so loud, and soon we hear more people singing. A crazy chorus of voices ringing out through the smoking trees. Hilariously defiant.

There's a type of humour people resort to in desperate situations, to make them more bearable. Already the fire has been christened the James Fire, named after a Saskatchewan government employee who answered the phone when someone called it in. I don't know where the government gets off sometimes, thinking they can name a natural disaster after someone who simply picks up the phone. Luke thinks we should name the fire after Bob Friendly, a back-to-the-lander who lives right next door to the Chervilles.

Earlier this afternoon Friendly was riding his quad on the edge of his pasture when a spark from the muffler ignited dead grass. Friendly stopped, tried to stomp it out, but the small fire zipped toward the dried-out spruce. The spruce caught like newspaper.

"It was running just like it was alive. That muffler's in terrible shape. I shoulda known better," he keeps telling everyone. No one disagrees with him.

Soon we're all calling it the Friendly Fire. I think about the four Canadians killed this spring near Kandahar. Violence dealt by the people you'd least expect. The previously benign forest fuelling destruction.

In its hunger for more trees, the fire forges its own wind, hissing sparks at us when we get too close to its heart. Jen and I douse our hair in water to stay cool and prevent the sparks from catching. The water courses down our dirty faces, creating a topographical map of rivers and streams. We've just resoaked ourselves for the third time when we hear a loud crack close to the clearing. I whip around just in time to see a dead poplar, broken by the fire-wind, topple onto a small group of people who were walking back to the clearing. Jen runs ahead, and after a stunned moment, I follow.

A small group of people circles someone lying on the ground. Dad, Will, and Sam are all staring down. Uncle Will rubs his left cheek, and when he pulls his hand away, it's bloody. He looks at it, momentarily confused, before he realizes that he has a gash on his face from a tree branch.

The group parts to let us in. It's Jack lying on the ground. Luke is crouched beside him. Jack's left arm looks strange, like something is trying to break through the skin. Luke touches it, and Jack yelps.

"You need to go to Turtleford. That arm's broken," Luke says.

"Jen, grab the first-aid kit from the one-ton. I can patch up Will."

Jen jogs off to get the first-aid kit. Luke kisses the top of my head and asks if I'll drive Jack to the hospital. "After all, he's your boss."

A couple hours later, Jack emerges from the Turtleford hospital with a cast on his arm. We stop at the Turtleford bar, buy a few cases of beer, and head north toward Brightsand Lake. I turn off the highway and onto a grid road just past the Turtleford cemetery so that Jack can open a beer. He passes me one too, and I accept it. Screw the law. I'm too tired to be good.

I crank up my stereo to drown out the rattle of my Jeep on the gravel just as the track switches to "Passenger Side" by Wilco. Nice coincidence. I harmonize with Tweedy.

"You're gonna make me spill my beer if you don't learn how to steer."

Jack snickers.

"So, where you staying tonight, Jack?"

"You know Ted Rogers? Lives north of Moosehead Hall?"

"Oh, yeah, known him forever."

"I'll crash with him. He'll be glad to see me and my beer."

We listen to the song, then the brief silence between tracks. Jack runs his hand along the dash.

"This is quite the truck, Darby. I haven't seen an AMC Jeep in a long time."

"Yeah, it's cool. Too bad it only gets ten miles to the gallon. And the vinyl bench seat's not the best. My legs always get stuck to it in the summer if I wear shorts." Even in the dark, I can see Jack's face pull up into a grin.

We decide to stop at the Moosehead School on the way to Ted's. I'm walking a tightrope, so tired and drained I'm afraid I'll tumble into a complete meltdown as soon as I stop moving. Jack says he'll need at least two more beers before he's ready to hang out with Ted.

Moosehead School sits in the middle of a small clearing on the north side of a grid road. The clearing is framed by a thick stand of poplar trees, their wilted leaves shivering in my headlights. I turn off the ignition and grab a flashlight from under the seat. The flashlight beam bounces off the sturdy green steps, lights up the white paint and green-trimmed windows of the neat, one-room schoolhouse.

Jack walks ahead of me, and I illuminate the path. He tries the door, looks back at me in surprise as it swings open.

"It's never locked," I say.

The paint inside is the same dark green as the exterior trim. A wall separates the entrance from the rest of the room. We walk into the main room, and I point the flashlight at the walls, spotlighting pictures of school alumni and children's artwork hanging above the chalk board. The chalk board itself is layered with signatures of previous visitors. *Joan Schmidt, Saskatoon, 2000.* Local high school kids have erased the names in the middle to make their own mark. *GARD 2002,* with a dozen names signed within the bubble letters. I wonder if the misspelling is intentional.

Something tickles the back of my neck, and I squeak involuntarily. Jack brushes at my neck. A large black spider with a fat white abdomen tumbles to the floor, attempts to scurry out of the flashlight beam. Jack squashes it with one stomp of his dirty Red Wing boots.

"That was a big sucker," he says. "Should rain now."

"We can only hope."

Three rows of desks face the teacher's desk. I sit on the teacher's desk, run my hands along the smooth wood, contemplating the two tiny desks at the front of the third row.

"My dad went to school here," I say. "In grade one he sat in one of those little desks."

"How old is your dad?"

"Real old. Turning fifty-two in November."

"Will went to school here, too," Jack says.

"How did you know that?"

"He carved his name into this desk." I amble over to the little desk Jack is looking at. Will Fletcher. Each letter straight and neat and precisely formed.

"He stayed with my Dad's family in the second part of grade two, along with his sisters. His dad had run off with another woman, and his mom, Jessie, nearly lost her mind. She couldn't handle the kids, couldn't even look after herself. She moved in with her sister, and Grandma and Grandpa took the kids. Uncle Will said it was the best seven months of his childhood."

"Shit."

"Yeah, my grandparents had their issues. Well, Grandma has her issues. Grandpa's pretty great. But they took being parents pretty serious. They tried real hard, and they could've done a lot worse." I think about that for a moment. I guess my parents were the same, even with all their faults.

"Anyway, that was the summer Dad and Will decided to get into the cattle business together. Crazy, hey?" I sit on the teacher's desk again.

"Persistent," says Jack.

Jack sits on the edge of the desk and offers me a beer. It's a little warm now, but I accept it gratefully. We start talking about growing up in small towns (Jack's originally from Biggar), about his divorce from Susan. Jack says he used to own a pub on Broadway in Saskatoon, and he worked a lot of nights.

Susan was lonely and had an affair with a high-school flame. Jack worked even more, not wanting to believe what was happening, so she divorced him. Before I know it, I'm telling him all about Luke.

"I'm not sure how we started dating. I always liked him, but more as a friend. After my mom died, I just kind of felt tired. Luke kept asking me out, and eventually I said yes. Luke made me feel safe. He always made me feel better when I was bummed out.

"After I flunked out of university I thought we'd break up. I thought about moving to Vancouver, starting a band. But I got scared. I couldn't imagine living on my own. Trying to find a job and pay the bills in a big city like Vancouver. So I moved home. Luke wanted to stick with me even though I was a failure. I knew I was lucky to be with a guy like him, so I stuck with him. Well, mostly, anyway. We've broken up a few times."

"Doesn't sound like a good reason to stay with someone."

"I know. But I don't want to hurt him. He's such a good guy..."

Somehow, as if by magic, the space between us has disappeared. We now sit close, side by side, our thighs touching.

And then, suddenly, we're kissing, and Jack's mouth tastes like smoke. I like the taste of smoke.

We strip messily. I try to help Jack pull his T-shirt over his cast, but quickly give up. Our clothes still cling to both of us as we push the books off the desk. The flashlight falls too, the beam of light bouncing against the walls before settling close to the floor.

# CHAPTER SIX

When my dad picked up his Fender Telecaster and took the stage, he was a different person. More than a rancher. It wasn't just the crisp black cowboy shirt with the white piping and embroidered red roses that he wore only for dances. It was more than the way he slicked back his hair, or the woody smell of his English Leather aftershave.

When Roy Swank's freshly polished cowboy boots hit that stage, he stood straighter, seemed looser and more energized at the same time. He fused himself to his guitar, and the music flowed from somewhere inside him.

Dad's band called themselves Roy Swank and the Dexter All-Stars. Dad played guitar, switching between his Fender and his acoustic, a Martin. He also sang, switching lead with Sam's mom, Ursula. People said it was like having Johnny Cash and Emmy Lou on the same stage.

The All Stars would play at all the little country halls and hockey rinks in the area — Pine Grove, Moosehead, sometimes venturing into Livelong or Turtleford or Walburg (hitting the big time, Dad joked). But their favourite was Dexter Hall, near Turtle Lake's north shore. Though Dexter could hold only about seventy-five people, the acoustics were perfect and every note rang clear. The hall got so full, and people danced so much, that sometimes they cracked the doors open in the winter. And if you were outside, you'd see the escaped heat clouding the area around the front door.

Roy Swank and the Dexter All-Stars were a real dance band. They played Texas swing, two-steps, a little rockabilly, waltzes. Ursula made the songs swing with the stand-up bass she'd crammed into her 1961 Falcon station wagon years ago when she left Ottawa for her first teaching contract in Andrew, Alberta.

"I didn't pack many clothes," she told people when they wondered how she managed to bring the bass out.

Marvin O'Conner had been playing with Dad since they were teenagers, and he still kept the beat. He deliberately played the snare behind the beat sometimes, giving some songs a subtle laid-back feel. When I first picked up on this, it felt like the world opened up to me a little. As though I'd been given a glimpse of how things worked.

Jen and Luke's grandpa, George Cherville, could play anything with strings, and so he'd pick the banjo and mandolin or saw the fiddle into song. He'd do a few Metis fiddle songs throughout the night, and Dad would yield the stage to him and waltz Mom around the hardwood.

Ross Cherville was the best dancer. He taught the kids the steps, but otherwise he would dance only with Lena. Everyone else switched dance partners frequently. Will danced all night and made a point of asking nearly every woman there for one turn on the hardwood. He always kissed his partner's hand at the end of the dance — very gallantly, I thought.

Bea never looked the least bit jealous, even if he kissed another woman on the cheek. Sometimes jealousy flashed on their husbands' faces — a slight snarl lifting the lip or the eyes narrowing into a brief glare. But they knew he meant nothing by it. Most of them didn't even cut in, but waited for the next song.

During the second set, George would swing into the Red River Jig. We'd form little circles of two or three or four or five on the dance floor. Ross would teach the kids the steps. Sam's older sister, Brenda, was always the best of the kids, partly because she had a few years on the rest of us. But this just made me and Jen try harder. By the time we were ten, our feet flashed.

The kids spent the night running around the adults' legs, or standing on Ross' feet as he taught us the waltz, two-step, and foxtrot. I wanted nothing more than to move to the music, to unlock the beat with my body, and I would dance myself to exhaustion, nearly falling asleep on my feet.

As the night wore me out, someone would carry me to the coat room. I'd slumber on a pile of fluffy winter coats, the scents of cologne and perfume still lingering on the collars and mingling in my nose.

And I'd dream of the day I'd make people move. Make them dance until they forgot about winter scratching at the door.

When my Dad gave me my first guitar, he told me, "A musician's style is a reflection of her personality."

"What do you mean?" I asked.

"Well, think of how your Grandma plays the piano. How would you describe it?"

I thought for a second. "It's almost perfect. She never makes a mistake."

"Yes, she's technically flawless. What else? Is that how you want to play?"

"I don't know." These were not topics I discussed with Grandma. Grandma, I suddenly realized, played sheet music as though it were a recipe not to be deviated from. And, though I loved her, I had to admit she viewed life the same way. Everything was clear, black and white. Add enough hard work and common sense, and you'd get the results you wanted in any situation. She'd as much as told me.

"Maybe not. I always know what she's going to do next. And it's kind of rigid."

"It's good to build up your chops, but you need to take chances sometimes. You need to bring your audience along with you for the ride. You need to let them see who you really are. Playing guitar is like surfing. You want to be at the edge of your ability, close to wiping out."

"But what if I do wipe out? I don't want to look stupid in front of a bunch of people."

"You will wipe out sometimes. But that's okay. The audience will forgive you."

I thought about musicians who played this way. Dad really liked Greg Keelor, and I realized this was why. His guitar solos were interesting, and no one cared that they weren't perfect.

Bob Dylan fell off the wave regularly, but the fall was always spectacular.

I was in love with Joan Jett at the time. She was straight-forward power. No bullshit.

Neil Young wasn't a technician, but his guitar and voice unwrapped life, revealing an emotional core.

Mavis Staples didn't play the guitar, but I could always hear pure love in her voice. "What about Jimi Hendrix? He's technically amazing, but he surfs, too."

Dad smiles. "Jimi isn't riding the wave. Jimi *is* the wave."

I wanted to be the wave.

I wasn't sure if I could be brave enough or good enough or inspired enough. But I could try.

I thought about this conversation all the time while I learned the guitar, studying the ideas that sprang from it as closely as I studied chord progressions. My piano playing loosened up, too. After a couple years even Grandma was impressed.

"I wish my playing were that fluid," she said to me one afternoon at the end of our lesson.

Once I asked Bea if an artist's personality showed up in her painting.

"Oh, yes," she said. "I think my personality, my whole world view, is encoded in my art. Often it's subconscious."

She pointed to a recently finished canvas. A large, rectangular piece.

"What do you think that piece says about me?" she asked.

I studied it carefully for several seconds before I spoke.

"Well, those are your horses. Last year's foals?" Bea nodded. "Well, at first it seems like a really high-energy, happy painting, you know. The foals are kicking and bucking and playing, and the mares are grazing nearby. That one mare is nuzzling her foal. And the sun is shining, and it's early spring. The leaves have just come out, they're almost fluorescent green, like they always are when they first emerge."

I kept looking, trying to figure out why the painting made me tense.

"But there's a storm coming. You can just see the thunderheads at the edge, there. And it's really windy. Look at how the trees are bent.

"And there's something wrong with that one foal. Look, it's by itself, and it looks listless. Its ears are kind of drooping. And even though it's a sorrel foal, you've added a blue undertone, so it looks sad. And its mother isn't around. That's weird. You'd think the mare might be worried about her foal.

"So what does this say about you? I don't know, but I think you're saying that first impressions don't tell the whole story."

Bea had been staring out the window, and her eyes were shiny and sad. I was suddenly afraid something was really wrong. "That little filly died last year," she said.

Then, suddenly, it was like she flipped a switch. She blinked hard, and her eyes lost their glassy look, and she smiled at me.

"Now, why don't you play me a little Neil Young? Hopefully my piano's not too out of tune."

I started splicing the idea of personality into almost everything related to music and band dynamics. It was the constant thread that ran through everything a band did, making each new album theirs, even as the band grew and their style changed.

It was the magic that made some bands brilliant, at least as important as the individual players' abilities, I thought one day. And it was also the dynamite that could blow a band to pieces.

Then, one day, somewhere in the winter of grade eight, the real danger of this approach hit me. It wasn't that I would make a technical mistake, which the audience might or might not notice. It was that I would lay it all out, let them see who I really was, and they would hate it. They would hate me and reject me.

It was like playing naked. Stripping off my skin so they could see the muscle, the blood, the bone of my music, and my self. How could I possibly think of doing that when I couldn't even put up my hand during math class?

I could not be brave, I decided. Much better to be safe.

Dad, Grandma, my band teacher, they all noticed the change in my playing right away.

"It's like you've burned out a light bulb up there," Mrs. Shevchenko cried, tapping my forehead.

She was tiny but she seemed much bigger, the way she threw her arms around. Her long brown hair filled up the air around her. Sometimes, when she thought students weren't paying attention, she'd swear under her breath. No one called her on it, though. We all loved her.

I looked at my feet while she ranted on in despair. But I didn't deviate from my plan, whether I was singing or playing piano or guitar.

Grandma and Dad were much more subtle. They didn't say a

thing, but I could see worry spread from the corners of their eyes.

Bea noticed too, of course. "Is everything okay at school?" she asked me one day, after I'd finished performing a Joni Mitchell song for her. I couldn't even let myself go in Bea's house, at her piano.

"Yeah, it's fine," I said. "I'm just having trouble hitting all the notes sometimes."

"You know, Darby, being an artist means you have to be brave. You have to cowboy up, Buttercup."

"I know, Aunty." I didn't change course, though.

Sometimes when no one was in the house, I'd climb the narrow steps to the attic and listen to Dad's old records and sing along. I'd channel every hurt and triumph I'd experienced so far into my voice, as only a melodramatic teenager can do. I'd sing like no one was listening, my voice a whitecap lunging at the shore.

But hiding my heart would keep rejection and disappointment from my front door, I thought. And so I went to church and sang in the choir with my grandma, even though sometimes I longed to pound out the devil's interlude on the church piano and channel Ozzy from my gut.

Secretly, I thought that if God is everywhere and every-thing, God and the devil must be the same creature, so why not celebrate the devil's music? But I didn't voice this thought.

Then Mom got sick.

I didn't realize she was sick right away. Mom and Dad didn't want to worry me at first, so they said they were taking a trip to Saskatoon to see Uncle George, who had hurt his back working construction.

"We trust you enough to stay home alone. If you need anything, call Bea and Will," Mom said. "And no parties."

It was right before the Christmas break, and so I threw a huge party. Kids from the St. Walburg, Edam, and Glaslyn high schools came. Gary Weaver and his friends got in a huge fight with some Edam boys and someone punched a hole in the living room wall (it was over hockey).

When Mom and Dad came home a few days later, they didn't even notice the hole at first. And when Dad finally did see it, Will came over and patched the drywall, and they repainted the whole living room. I didn't even get grounded.

I thought that was strange, but kind of great.

Mom also came home with a whole bunch of crystals. She didn't say anything about them, but in the mornings she'd sit at the kitchen table holding a crystal in each hand. Sometimes she'd have one by her feet. She'd sit that way for several minutes, her eyes closed.

I thought that was a little weird, too. Mom had never been into that New Age-y stuff. In fact, she'd argued with Ursula about stuff way tamer than crystals.

The next Sunday, she came to church with me and Grandma and Dad, to watch me sing, she said. That's when I knew something was wrong. Before that, she'd only watched me at the Easter Cantata.

After the service, as we were about to climb into her Subaru, she touched my arm and said, "Darby, I have leukemia. But I'm going to be okay. I'm going to fight it as hard as I can." Worry lined her forehead.

"Are you scared?" I asked.

"Yes." Her face crumpled like balled-up looseleaf paper, and she hugged me so hard she forced the air from my lungs. And we cried in the church parking lot, not giving a shit about stoicism or any of that other crap.

My mom hung on to life by her fingernails.

One February day, she had Bea and Lena over for coffee.

"Those fucking crystals were a waste of money," she said. And suddenly she stood up, marched to her bedroom, and came out with a box of crystals.

She stood in the verandah door throwing them, one at a time, as far as she could into the yard. Bea and Lena and I stared at each other for a moment, stunned. Then Bea went to her and started throwing crystals, too. Then Lena joined in.

Afterwards they all sat on the steps, laughing and sobbing. Their tears froze on their skin. By now Mom's hair, eyelashes, and eyebrows were gone, and she looked like a newborn baby.

I made more coffee for them, then went up to my room.

Mom had always put her faith in science, in technology, and in willpower, but it wasn't enough. It wasn't saving her. And it couldn't tell her what came next, other than physical decay.

She kept coming to church, at first so she could see me sing in the choir. But after the crystal failure she started talking to the pastor a little after the services. And sometimes I would catch her praying. She was praying for her life, and I was praying for her life, too.

It didn't work. It didn't work at all.

Mom grew thinner and weaker, and no matter how much poison the doctors pumped into her, they couldn't beat back the cancer. She often stayed after church services so the pastor could pray over her. But soon she didn't have the strength to sit through the services.

I begged God to save her. I would do anything. Anything.

Winter thawed and spring pushed the first green from the ground and the brown tree branches. I rode Magic across the road to Bea and Will's, and wandered for hours through the trails and pastures, ever vigilant even in my grief because Magic would just as soon throw me as let me ride with her.

I rode until the sun started to sink, then turned for home. We stopped on Crocus Hill, a south-facing ridge overlooking poplar and spruce and pine, and in the distance, Brightsand Lake. The crocuses had popped through last year's dead grass and were already starting to fade.

Magic snorted and flew sideways. I tightened the rein on the snaffle bit, took her head away, and kicked out her hip. In the swampy valley below, a moose crashed through the bush.

How can the world hold so much beauty and be so fucking shitty at the same time, I wondered. I was so angry I felt like I was about to explode into a million burning stars, incinerating the entire forest.

"Fuck! Fuck, fuck, fuck, fuck!"

Magic ripped the rein from my hand and started to run for home. I leaned forward a little and loosened the reins. I didn't give a shit if I got hurt or if she broke her wind or took a wrong step. I wanted to run her until all the rage left my body, until we reached some kind of end.

Three days later, we took Mom to the Royal University Hospital in Saskatoon. She died there.

A few weeks after she died, I phoned Grandma and told her I was quitting the choir. Grandma hung up on me. It's the only time she ever did that to me, though she and Mom hung up on each other many times over the years.

Dad didn't really want me to quit the choir, but he was never religious. He came to church only to see me sing, so we both stopped going.

My loss of faith wasn't an act of courage, though. I didn't fight for it. I let it slip away as easily as wind blows away loose soil. I never challenged God, never challenged the pastor. Or myself. I didn't rip my faith down and rebuild something stronger. I was too afraid of what that would look like, what it would take out of me or reveal about me.

But there was always something in me like water running during the spring melt. No matter how hard I tried to control and block it, it would find a way through. It would erode the earth, burst the dam, or simply flow around the rock.

And so I wrote songs.

Sometimes I'd start noodling around on my guitar, playing with chord progressions. Then I would hum along, trying to figure out the melody. Finally I would start thinking of words and slowly fold and unfold the lyrics into the melody until everything fit.

Other times I would write down chunks of lyrics, arrange and re-arrange words until a rhythm emerged. I would read things out loud to figure out how the song should flow, then sing it, then wrap the music around it.

The songs never came easily at the right times. Instead, lyrics or melody would materialize while I was driving, or riding a green colt, or studying for chemistry, or in the middle of a dream. And if I wasn't able to write it down immediately, or play the first notes on my guitar, the bulk of it disappeared into the ether again, and I would sit down later and try to dig it out of thin air.

"Fuck this," I would think, but I'd keep pawing at the air because to deny it was a kind of death.

The more I worked at it, though, the more the muse graced me. Sometimes I would sit in the attic for hours, watch dawn edge up through the east windows. Mom had always nagged me to go to bed at a reasonable time, but Dad was a laissez-faire parent, so I could dedicate time to my obsession when it beckoned me.

Most of my early stuff was garbage. I hated it so much I couldn't stand to even play it after I'd finished it, or given up on it. It was so far below the bar set by the musicians I loved that I almost felt ashamed. And I didn't share it with anyone.

But every now and then I'd write a song that sort of hung together. It wasn't a masterpiece, and it didn't quite sound the way it felt in my marrow, but it was in the same township, at least.

I could never bring myself to perform the songs, at least not at first. But I'd write out the lyrics, chord progressions, and melody and give them to Mrs. Shevchenko for feedback.

"Darby, it seems lovely, but I can't possibly tell you anything until you play this for me," she'd say. "I need to hear what you're going to put into it."

And so, one spring day in grade twelve, I stayed after school and caught her before she left for the day. And we went to the band room, right next door to the kindergarten class, and I sat down at the old bench piano.

"Go ahead," said Mrs. Shevchenko. "You won't gain anything by not risking something."

My fingers grazed the oil film on the piano keys. I slowly breathed in and out, thought of how I'd felt the nights I wrote this song. The best I had so far. I wasn't sure that it was much.

The melody was kind of a rip-off of "I'm Always in Love," by Wilco, which I'd just heard three weeks earlier, when I picked up *Summerteeth*. I'd listened to it so many times it'd seeped into my bones.

*The sky mourned for three weeks.*
*Thick grey pressed down on me.*
*Rain drowned my sunshine laughs*
*And carved through my cheeks.*

*Everything I've known has blown away like chaff*
*And I'm afraid I can't get it back.*
*I'm worried I can't get it back, can't get it back.*

*I watched the sun rise,*
*Fire in the sky,*
*And I saw it set in your eyes.*
*And I'll never bring you back.*

*And I'll never get it back.*
*I can't it back. Can't get it back.*

I sat there, an eroded knoll, waiting for Shevchenko to rain criticism on me, both caring desperately and not caring at all what she had to say.

"Fuck," said Mrs. Shevchenko. "Why've you been holding out on us?"

I exhaled.

"I was afraid and I didn't know what else to do."

And suddenly I wanted to be the wave again.

# CHAPTER SEVEN

*The forest is dark. Shaggy black spruce stretch toward the sky, blocking out the moonlight. For a moment, I lose all sense of direction. Everything around me is spinning. I stand still until the ground stabilizes.*

*Mud sucks at my feet as I trudge through the muskeg. Something is wrong here. Every muscle in my body is on edge. I feel like I'm being watched. Stalked. The spruce are too close. I walk into a branch, and old man's beard brushes my face. I swat at the lichen, but it seems to cling to my face and hands.*

*Something smells putrid. Rancid meat and rotting garbage. The stench makes me gag. It's crashing through the bush, running toward me. Not even trying to be stealthy now.*

*I run.*

*A huge wind comes up, bending the spruce toward the ground. They reach for me, try to hold me still. I swat at their branches with an animal's desperation.*

*It's almost impossible to run through the muskeg. Ground that looks solid is not — it's like someone is pulling the rug from under my feet. I keep falling, sometimes in water up to my waist. Whatever is chasing me is getting closer, fast. I lunge forward.*

*Without warning, the forest ends. The wind stops. The ground is solid, dry, sandy. The black spruce give way to jack pine edged around a meadow. A narrow ridge rises up in the middle of the clearing. An esker. The esker at Brightsand Lake.*

*The thing is coming up behind me. I can hear it breathing now, long, ragged breaths. Impossibly loud.*

*I scurry up the esker. There are train tracks running along the top.*

*I dig deep, sprint. My lungs are bellows, pushing air into a coal-fired engine.*

*The tracks vibrate with each step of the thing behind me. Then they start shaking hard. That's when I realize the train is coming.*

*I look up just in time to see the train's headlight bearing down on me. I try to scream, but I can't force the scream out, no matter how hard I try.*

I wake up, still trying to scream, but only managing to moan. It's light out now. Early, early morning.

I don't want to face Luke. I've done this to him before, but it feels worse this time.

I need coffee.

As I wait for the coffee to brew, I pick up the messages. Several from the cops. They want to talk to me and Dad. Fuck sake. I don't write them down. We know the number anyway.

After coffee and a shower, I freshen up the music on my MP3 player. I need something more upbeat, so I fill it with my favourite Motown tunes. The Supremes, the Temptations, Smokey Robinson. Then I decide to add some Louis Armstrong and Frank Sinatra. Finally, I top it off with the Neville Brothers and Mavis Staples.

I feel better now. Calm and collected. I should go back to help with the fire. Luke might start to worry about me. Besides, I feel like I should help.

As I approach the Dexter Hall road, I see that there's a barricade and an RCMP car. Karin Polley gets out as I stop. I roll my window down.

"We're not letting any traffic through, with the fire," she says.

"Well, I'm going to help fight the fire. I was there last night."

"Just a minute, Darby." She walks to the patrol car, speaks into the radio before coming back.

"We'll let you through, but Sergeant Steele wants to talk to you first."

"Like, right now? Here?"

"Yes. She'll be here in a few minutes. She's just finishing up at the Cherville house."

"Okay, fine." Damn, they're persistent. Like a pitbull with a chicken, I think.

Steele comes barrelling down the road in a truck, much too fast even for me, and brakes hard as she approaches the road-block.

"Saskatoon drivers," I mutter, and Karin smirks despite herself.

Steele eases the pickup to the shoulder of the road, emerges from the driver's side, and beckons me over before climbing back in. I shuffle to the truck, dragging my toes in the dust and gravel, and slowly climb into the passenger's side.

Steele looks tired. The corners of her mouth are turned down, and she has dark circles under her eyes.

"Darby, tell me about your aunt's accident last fall," she says quietly.

"What are you talking about?"

"Last October your father drove Bea to the emergency room in Lloydminster. She had several cracked ribs. Tell me what happened."

I close my eyes, try to remember October. Try to remember if Dad and Bea went to Lloydminster. Nothing.

"I don't remember that. I went to Saskatoon the weekend after Thanksgiving to see a concert with Luke. Wide Mouth Mason."

Steele flips through her notebook, reads a scrawl so messy it looks like hieroglyphics to me. "That Friday your Dad drove Bea to the emergency room."

Fuck, I think. No one around here tells me anything. "I didn't know about it."

"You didn't notice anything when you got home? You didn't notice that Bea was in pain?"

"No." I think. "She asked me to ride some colts for her, but I did that a lot anyway. She got a migraine earlier that month, but she had a lot of those."

"Where was Will?"

"Did you ask him where he was?" I shoot back, suddenly offended by the implication.

"Yes. Now I'm asking you. Again." She doesn't raise her voice, but each syllable is clipped. "Where was your uncle when all this was going on?"

"I don't know. He was around, I think."

"Then why didn't he drive her to the emergency room?"

"Once again, probably a question for Will."

"So, you're saying he was at the farm that weekend?"

"Well, I wasn't there that weekend, so I don't really know, do I? Apparently I know fuck all about any of this."

Steele says nothing for at least two minutes. She just stares at me. I stare back. Finally, she ends the silence.

"Darby, I have a hard time believing that you didn't know your uncle was beating your aunt."

This time, I say nothing. I can't believe they think that. They're wasting their time on my uncle while Bea's real killer is out there. Fucking stupid cops.

But then a chill runs through my body, and I wonder, for a moment, whether it could be true.

No. Steele's playing mind games with me.

"Why the hell do you think that?"

"Your uncle can't account for his whereabouts that weekend. He claims he wasn't home, but he's lying. We pulled the hospital records from Lloydminster and Turtleford, and your aunt has been to the emergency room at least ten times in the last ten years. Your mom, your dad, or Lena Cherville always took her. Never Will. Will's alibi for your aunt's murder isn't holding up, either. Your dad is trying to cover for him, but he's not doing a very good job. I don't think he really wants to cover for him. I'm one hundred percent sure Will did it, and we're going to arrest him for it."

She recites the facts in that same calm voice, but all the gentleness is gone. She thinks I'm part of this.

"Do you even need me? You obviously have all the answers."

"Darby, your uncle killed your aunt. Think carefully about whose side you're going to take in this."

"I'm on my family's side," I say. "I don't think you can force me to keep talking to you."

"Not right now, but you should think about whether you want to be charged with obstruction. Because I will charge you, your father, and anyone else I have to if that's what it takes to get you people to talk."

"Fuck. Charge me with whatever the hell you want. I can't tell you what I don't know."

Steele closes her notebook. "You know more than you think you do, Darby. I'm trying to help you."

"No, I don't! And no, you're not! Go to hell!" I slam the truck door.

Karin waves me through. As I drive by, she briefly makes eye contact with me, gives me a slight nod. Then she glances toward Steele, as though she's afraid of getting caught. She's an open book, I think.

When I pull into the yard, the first person I see is Lena, talking into a walkie-talkie. She's set up her yard as command central and is coordinating the volunteer firefighters. She looks calm and focused. Maybe the police haven't interrogated her yet today, but then I see Cardinal and the other Major Crimes detective leaving the house. They walk right by Lena, and she waves briefly. They've already talked to her, I'm sure.

I feel like a bag of raw nerves.

Mom always said Lena was the best person to have in the emergency room, said it was her cold Swedish blood.

When Lena got the job as hospital administrator, Mom stopped talking to her briefly. But eventually Mom conceded Lena was the right woman for that job, too.

The weird thing is that I'd never thought of what kind of nurse my mother was until after she died. I assumed she treated her patients the same way she often treated me: with an impatient tolerance.

But after she died, her former patients flooded me with gratitude for her. It started at the funeral and continued for months afterwards.

"She fought for me," said one old woman from Thunderchild. "She's the one who knew I was having a heart attack. The doctors didn't believe me."

"She taught me how to get a handle on my diabetes," said a middle-aged man.

They went on and on, and their gratitude should have made me feel better. But I felt bitter. How could she spot pain in others so easily but miss it in her own family?

But now I know I was the one oblivious to everyone else's pain.

A few months after Mom died, Dad bought Bucky for me from the local horse trader, Jake Bennett. Bucky wasn't even halter broke, so Jake sold him for three hundred dollars.

"His name is Bucky. Bea will help you break him in," Dad said.

"Bucky? Does he buck?"

"Probably. Just don't look at the ground or that's where you'll end up."

We kept Bucky in the corral at Will and Bea's that winter. At first he was so skittish that he whirled away from me every time I approached, threatening to kick with his hind legs. If I got any closer, he'd take a swing, then race around the pen, crow-hopping and snorting.

By this time I'd ridden lots of green horses. Bea would put the first ten or so rides on a colt, and then, if he was going okay, I'd start riding him. I'd helped her halter-break the babies, too, but I'd never worked with an unhandled two-year-old.

But Bea was painting, manically, so I couldn't seek her help right away. Bea wasn't bipolar, but she would go through these periods where she'd spend every minute she could on her art, working through the night and barely eating. Will would usually cook for himself during these times, and Bea seemed to live on plain bread and air.

Eventually a multi-day migraine would crash down on her.

I don't know what set her off. I could never figure out a pattern to her frantic work periods. Sometimes she'd go months before another one would set in. Other times they hit one after the other for weeks. I could tell it was starting because she wouldn't look at me when I was talking to her, but behind me or over my head. As though she were watching for a storm on the horizon. And she didn't really listen to what anyone was saying, which was out of character for her.

Once the cycle began, it was impossible to interrupt it. And she was so productive that it seemed wrong to try to stop it, even though we all knew what was coming next. Her painting was raw emotion splashed on the canvas during these times.

Bea was in the early stages of such an episode when we dropped Bucky off in the corral that November. I tried to work him in the round pen the way Bea did, but he wouldn't hook on to me. Instead of turning to look at me, he just ran in circles endlessly, and I worried he'd catch cold from getting sweated up. I couldn't read his body language the way Bea did. I couldn't communicate.

So after a couple days, I decided the only solution was to bribe him with oats.

Bucky took the bait quickly, and over the next couple weeks he gradually allowed me to touch his head while he filled his face. Soon I could rub my hands down his back, pat his neck, and even lift his tail. But I was hesitant to pick up his feet. I was afraid he'd kick me square in the face.

Bea, meanwhile, was working up to her migraine. About twenty days after Bucky arrived, she finally crashed, literally.

I was in the kitchen taking a coffee break from Bucky when I heard something fall upstairs, in Bea's studio. I ran up the stairs and found Bea crouched on the floor, doubled over in pain, grasping her head.

Behind her was a huge canvas. It was the colour of bruises — dark purple and black. Bea had been using a knife to scrape away the fresh purple paint, revealing a blood-red undercoat. In some places, it looked like she'd been using her fingernails to gouge at the topcoat.

It was ugly and painful to look at and it made the hair on my arms stand up. I didn't like it at all.

Bea struggled to her feet. Black and dark purple paint covered her hands and wrists. It bruised her temples and the sides of her face where she'd been clawing at her head. It stuck to her hair like clots of old blood.

She looked like she'd lost a very bad fight.

"I'm okay," she said as she staggered to the bathroom. The door slammed behind her and she began retching.

I didn't know what to do. Usually Mom would help Bea, but Mom was dead, and this was Bea's first migraine since Mom had died. And Will and Dad were gone all week at Agribition in Regina.

I brought Bea a huge pitcher of water. She wouldn't drink it. She wouldn't leave the bathroom.

"The cold tiles feel good," she said, stretching out beside the toilet. "I'm glad I cleaned the bathroom yesterday."

"Do you need some Tylenol or something?"

She laughed bitterly.

"I'll never keep it down. And it wouldn't work, anyway."

I stayed and fretted for a couple hours.

"Go home," Bea said. "It's out of your control."

The next morning, I skipped school to take care of Bea. She had made it to bed. Her bedroom curtains were drawn, and she had an eye mask over her eyes. I emptied the yellow bile out of the bucket beside her bed, brought her more water, and went outside to work with Bucky. I checked on her several times that day, emptied the bucket, and brought more water.

The third day I checked on Bea first thing in the morning. She was already sitting at the kitchen table, in her housecoat, very slowly eating a piece of plain toast and drinking water. She smelled like bubble bath and shampoo. Her skin was still pale, but her eyes were focused.

"Thank you for taking care of me," she said. "Now go to school."

After school I stopped by again. She wanted to see how I was doing with Bucky, so we went outside, even though the weak winter sunlight was dying.

By now I basically had him halter broke, and he even liked to have his face scratched. But I was still afraid to touch his feet.

Bea looped a soft rope around his left front leg. Bucky didn't flinch. She ran the rope up and down each leg, and he never threatened to kick.

"You need to get him used to having his feet handled," Bea lectured, running her hands down his front left leg. Bucky lifted his foot.

"You need to be able to do this all the time. Not just pick up his foot, but touch his whole leg. His whole body. You need to know what's normal, so you can check if something's wrong, if he's in pain."

"Well, won't he just limp if he's in pain, anyway?"

"No. I thought you knew better than that." Bea set Bucky's foot down, and looked at me as though I'd just crawled out from under a rock.

"What? I mean, I know you need to clean out their feet and stuff, but they'll tell you if they're in pain, won't they?"

"No, Darby, a horse will hide pain if he can. He's a prey animal, so he hides his injuries from predators. You need to be able to feel if something's wrong. Heat, tension, the swish of a tail, or the slightest flinch can mean something's wrong."

"Oh, I didn't know they did that."

"Of course they do. Just like people." Bea bent over again, running her hands down Bucky's leg. This time he didn't move until she grasped his hoof and gently lifted it.

I thought about the last three weeks, about Bea's painting, about the migraine. I was missing something. It was like sitting in a boat and watching jackfish swimming. You can never figure out exactly where they are because of the way the light bends when it hits the surface.

Lena waves me over and starts filling me in on the latest news as she hands me bottled water and tuna sandwiches.

"The government firefighters are here now. They've set up camp on the other side of the lake. But they're focused on protecting the cabins and keeping the fire out of the provincial forest. We need every volunteer we can to protect the farms and houses around here."

I'm about to ask Lena about the cops, but Luke pulls up in the water truck and starts refilling the tank with a garden hose.

"Everyone's working near the golf course right now. Luke'll give you a ride out."

I climb into the truck next to Luke and look over at him. He has no idea that anything is wrong, that I've betrayed him again. And I know that I can get away with it — if I want to. If I stay away from Jack for a while, this will all disappear.

"How's it going?" I ask.

"Not good. How's Jack?"

"Okay. Just the broken arm."

Over the next several days, I don't leave the Cherville farm. I develop a routine. I wake up, sometimes before dawn. No matter how early it is, Luke is already fighting the fire. I get dressed, usually in the same filthy clothes from the day before, and go downstairs. Luke's great-aunt Louise has lost her house and is staying with them. She always has coffee ready for me, so strong the spoon stands up. I wonder if she's related to Will somehow.

We drink coffee together, and I eat a bit of toast. Then I fill up my water bottle and go wherever Lena tells me to go and work until I'm dead tired.

I start losing weight. I don't know how much, exactly, but after five days my jeans keep falling off, so I borrow one of Jen's belts. The weight loss doesn't look good on me. I was thin enough to start with, and now I look like a broken-down old mare.

Fighting the fire feels surreal, partly because of the physical exhaustion. But it's just weird, too. The fire goes underground, chewing through tree roots and peat, only to pop up where we least expect it. We're constantly scurrying between these hot spots. People keep saying the fire can smoulder underground for weeks and months.

I want to believe they're bullshitting me, but I don't know.

Dad and Will stay with Bob Friendly. Every couple of days one of them goes home to check on the cattle. I don't see them every day, so when I do see them, I'm surprised by how terrible they look. The cut on Will's face doesn't seem to be healing, but he won't go to a doctor. It might be the smoke and ash, but his skin looks grey and shiny and swollen, as though it's about to split.

Dad, on the other hand, is wasting away like me. After a week, his cheekbones are jutting out of his skin.

Will talks non-stop to whoever will listen. He talks about how much he misses Bea. He misses her laugh, he misses her cooking, he misses how she'd talk about art, even getting into one-sided arguments with him about it ("I'm not arguing with you," he'd say). He misses the way she made coffee.

I can't see there's much trick to that one. She just poured tons and tons of coffee into the filter. But I miss having coffee with her. The way she'd hold the mug in both hands like she was trying to warm herself, even in the summer.

Her garden has gone to hell and the colts aren't getting started and Wilson, her old dog, won't eat, Will says.

Will says he doesn't understand why the cops keep harassing him instead of looking for her killer. They keep showing up at Friendly's at all hours of the night, trying to talk to Will. They want to know where Bea was going, but how should Will know? She had some kind of secret, Will said. She was keeping something from him.

"She got herself tangled up in something, I don't know what. But whatever it is, it got her killed. And now I'm left here to deal with it," he says.

"You know who they should talk to is that preacher in Mervin. The one who did the service. She hung out with him a little too much for my comfort," he adds. Friendly and the other men gathered around nod wisely. Dad is silent.

"Must be easy to make you uncomfortable," I snort. Will glares at me.

I pick up my shovel and walk back to the fire.

Will and I are hauling five-gallon pails of water to pour on the fire one morning in mid-July when Dad comes marching into the bush.

"Will, we need to move the commercial herd," Dad says.

"Why? They out of pasture again?"

"Something killed one of your calves."

"Goddammit!" Will throws the empty pail to the ground.

At first Dad won't say what did it. "Can't say for sure," he keeps saying.

"Roy, will you just spit it out," Will finally barks.

"A bear," Dad says reluctantly.

"We've never had a problem with bears," Will says. "Are you sure it wasn't coyotes? Or wolves?"

"It wasn't coyotes. The calf's back was broke. And the carcass was drug into the bush."

"Jesus Christ, this goddamned drought," Will grumbles.

"What?" I say, confused. Bears eating calves? What does the drought have to do with it? Then I think, the bears must be starving. No berries, no forage.

Dad and Will discuss their next move. Will wants to hunt down the bear right now, but Dad says they'll never track it now. The calf has been dead for a while — Dad thinks a day. They decide to call the local conservation officers, to see if they'll set a live trap for the bear. But the cows need to be moved.

We all drive home immediately. Dad and I catch and saddle our horses and lope the short distance to Will's farm. I haven't ridden Bucky in two weeks, and he crow-hops a few times.

I pull Bucky's head up before he can really start bucking and dig my heels into his sides. He lunges into a full-out gallop, and we race by Dad.

"Yee-ha!" Dad whoops as his white mare, Booter, breaks into a run.

I wasn't always so casual about Bucky's crow-hopping. Actually, if Bea were here, she would probably give me hell for urging him to run instead of making him settle down.

When Bea and I were starting Bucky, I tried to talk Bea into riding him first.

"He's your horse, Darby. And you can do it. Just stay calm, stay balanced, and don't let him get his head down. If he tries to buck, pull his head around and kick his hip out. Disengage his hindquarters. He can't buck while he's crossing over with his back feet," she said.

I spent a lot of time disengaging Bucky's hindquarters while Wilson, still in late puppyhood, lay outside the corral, watching our every move.

"Almost everything worth doing in life is hard," Bea said when I complained about the slow progress. "Keep working with him and he'll get there. Just try not to get bucked off, or he'll think he's won and it'll be harder."

Even though we're a few miles from the fire, the hazy air burns my eyes. I suddenly wonder if it's needling into Bucky's lungs as he runs. I shift my weight back, and he slows just a little.

As we get closer to Will's yard, Dad and I pull our horses down to an easy lope, then a trot. Will is waiting for us by the barn. His stallion, Horse, is saddled and pawing the ground.

Wilson comes down from the house, barks at us twice, then shuffles back to the deck.

Jesus, he's all sack and ribcage, I think. Out loud, I say to Dad, "He's really not eating."

"He's sure not," Dad says.

Horse neighs shrilly at us or, most likely, at Dad's mare, Booter. Horse is technically a palomino quarter horse, but he's not the warm gold colour that most people associate with palominos. His coat is a pale yellow, like he's been bleached by the sun. And he's mean as hell. He'll bite or strike other horses whenever he gets a chance, and he'll go after people sometimes, too. I guess some stallions are like that, but I don't know why Will bothers riding him when he's got plenty of others to choose from.

He's such an ugly colour that I don't understand why people

pay his stud fee, either. He won some cutting horse competitions years ago, but there's no way I'd want one of his progeny.

"They'll be a bitch to bring in the hotter it gets today, so let's get moving." Will swings up into the saddle, and we all trot west, to the Crocus Hill pasture. It's a rugged swath of land, full of steep hills, swamps, and bush. I hope the cows are ready to move.

Many of the cows are in the clearing near the fence line. They're nervous, mooing at their calves constantly. One cow has gashes on her face, as though she was slapped by the bear. She keeps bawling for her dead calf.

The three of us bring more cows and calves out of the bush, slowly herding them into the clearing with the rest of the herd. Most of the cows just graze the dusty grass, but one older Black Angus cow keeps looking toward the bush. Her yellow ear tag reads J57.

"Don't do it, J57," I growl, tucking her into the middle of the herd before I ride off to gather more cattle.

We finish gathering the cows in an hour or so. Will and Dad do a head count, confirming that we have them all. We start pushing the herd along the fence line. Dad rides directly behind them, and I ride to the side of them, to keep them along the fence. Will is a little way in front of me.

Old J57 is right beside me, still looking for an escape. She trots ahead of me, and I nudge Bucky into a fast walk. J57 looks back at her calf. Then she breaks into a clumsy gallop, her milk bag swinging like a pendulum, and blows right by us. Her calf and four other cow–calf pairs follow her into the bush.

"Shit! Shit, shit, shit!" Bucky shifts his weight to his hind legs, whirls around, and follows them at a run. As we enter the bush, I pull Bucky up, worried about tripping over deadfall or getting clotheslined by a branch. The bush is so thick here that normally we wouldn't be able to see the cows, but the drought has killed a lot of the vegetation. I can see the cows crashing through the underbrush, unstoppable as tanks, their calves trotting behind them.

Some people say cows are stupid, that the smart ones are shipped instead of being kept as breeding stock. They haven't met J57. J57 leads her small band of rebels under low-hanging branches and into thick underbrush, forcing me to duck and go around and constantly slow down as I protect my face from the branches. Bucky is pulling at the bit, frustrated by our slow pace. We are gradually gaining on them, but it's taking forever.

The cows spook at something and go tearing through the bush as though a pack of wolves are nipping their heels. Bucky suddenly shies at something on the ground. I only get a glimpse of shredded carcass, but I know it must be the calf. It smells like rotting meat and fermenting grass. Thank God the bear's not here.

Finally, J57 miscalculates, and we all break into a small clearing. Bucky rushes around and in front of the cows, stopping them before they can duck back into the bush. J57 studies us, then makes a break for the bush she came from. Bucky cuts her off quickly, and we herd them onto a wide trail that goes back toward the fence line.

By now it's hot as hell. The smoke is making Bucky and the cattle cough. It must be close to noon. Sweat is running down my back, and my face is scratched raw.

I think of "Ghost Riders in the Sky," the old country standard. So this is what eternity is like for bad cowboys.

J57 is persistent in her escape attempts. She dashes for the bush every chance she gets. The other cows have given up and saunter down the trail no matter what J57 is doing. J57's escapades are making me grouchy, although I think Bucky enjoys the chase. He always has one or both ears forward, pointed at J57, as though he's watching her every move. He seems to know that she's about to run before I do, and cuts her off before she's even off the trail. As he turns her back onto the trail, he lays his ears flat, as though telling her to stay the hell out of the bush.

"Good horse, Bucky," I say, patting his neck, and his right ear flicks back to catch my voice.

When we reach the fence line, the rest of the herd is a few hundred feet ahead of us, and our little group of cows trots to catch up, their calves bucking and kicking beside them. Bucky and I trot beside them to make sure they don't break into the bush again, but even J57 seems to have given up. The heat has taken all her fight away.

Dad and Booter are still pushing the herd from behind. All five cows trot right past them, into the herd, and Dad nods at me as Bucky trots past. Up ahead, Will is cursing at Horse and booting him in the sides. Suddenly Horse lunges ahead and begins bucking, hard. Will lasts one, two bucks, then flies forward, right over Horse's head and onto the hard ground. He tucks his head and hits with his shoulder, rolling. I ride up to make sure he's not hurt.

"You all right, Uncle Will?"

"Jesus Christ, Darby, where the fuck were you?" He slowly stands up. His face is shiny red and tight, like an overcooked hotdog.

All the frustration of digging his livestock out of the bush boils over.

"I was chasing your fucking cows through the bush. And you're welcome, by the way."

Will's tone changes from accusing to pleading.

"I'm sorry, Darby. I lost it there. Could you grab my horse for me, please?"

"Catch him yourself." Before Will can say another word, I lope past him to catch another small group of cows meandering toward the bush. As soon as they see me coming, they turn back to the fence line, and I slow to a walk.

Everyone gets frustrated by cows sometime. Even my dad, who is probably the most patient person I know, swears at them.

Growing up, no one swore in the house, and my parents normally didn't let any curses slip around me. But when we were working with cattle, even I was allowed to swear. I used to savour this freedom and try to come up with the crudest, most creative strings of swear words I could imagine.

But no one ever swears at another person. It's a family rule that keeps one person's frustration from hurting others.

Once, when I was about thirteen, I swore at my mom when a cow got past her. I didn't really mean to do it; it just slipped out.

As soon as I said it, I felt terrible. And powerful, because for once I'd hurt my mom instead of the other way around.

My dad was so mad at me, he grounded me for a week. It was one of the few times he actually yelled at me, and I cried. Bea and Will were helping us that day, and after we were done, Will pulled me aside and told me I should treat my mother with more respect.

So I'm pissed off at Will not just because he swore at me while I was doing him a favour, but also because he broke our family rule. No one breaks that rule. And I don't understand how he could lose control of his anger, then regain it so quickly. He changed so fast it was like flipping a coin. I can't help thinking that he swore at me deliberately, to hurt me.

We herd the cows into a small pasture, with hay, that funnels into the corrals. It's all within sight of Will and Bea's house.

"Now that they're in, we might as well vaccinate the calves," Dad says. "We should have done it three weeks ago anyway."

"Tomorrow. Need to get that beat-up cow in to the vet first," Will says.

I sleep the rest of the afternoon, get up around supper to eat two boxes of Kraft Dinner, then sleep the rest of the night.

The next morning I wake up at dawn. Dad's already drinking coffee downstairs.

"We're vaccinating the calves today," he says. "Tomorrow

morning we'll move them to the south pasture. No grass left here anyway."

I nod.

Some of the neighbours are waiting for us at the corrals, and they help separate cows from calves. Once the calves are sorted and in the corral, I set up my vaccination area. I take a clean needle and syringe, fill it with liquid vaccine, and push the extra air out. Then I set the syringe so it delivers the exact same dose every time. I also like to have extra needles and syringes nearby, just in case a needle gets bent or something. There's always shit flying around, so I also have sani-wipes and a pail of diluted bleach to sterilize the needle.

I've always liked vaccinating. It takes a little bit of skill, and I'm pretty good at it. It also means I don't have to push calves down the laneway. The calves kick the pushers in the shins, and it hurts like hell.

Sam and his older brother take turns pushing the calves down the narrow laneway to the squeeze chute. It's tough work, especially this year. Because we're late doing it, the calves are bigger than usual. As the calf walks into the squeeze chute, Dad pulls a lever that closes the gate of the chute on the calf's neck and tightens around the body.

Dad punches a tag into the calf's ear. Because this is the commercial herd, not the purebred, they're not keeping any bulls for breeding, so all the bull calves are castrated.

I vaccinate on the neck, just under the skin. The trick is to grab a bit of skin and slide the needle into the little bundle at a bit of an angle. Usually this is easier to do on bigger calves, as they seem to have looser skin on the neck. I'm careful that I don't go too deep and hit the muscle. I also watch that I don't puncture the skin on the other side of the bundle, and squirt the vaccine into the air. The calves squirm and struggle in the chute, making what should be a relatively easy task difficult.

We all try to work quickly and carefully so that the calf isn't in the chute too long. Once we're done, the chute is loosened and the gate opened so the calf can rejoin its mother in the small pasture.

We take a short break at noon. Ursula has sent sandwiches with Sam. She's wrapped them in wax paper. She's the only one I know who still does that. The paper feels cold and crisp after sitting in the cooler for a few hours, and eating my cucumber sandwich is like biting into a cold spring. Perfect.

Sam is sitting by himself on the tailgate of his truck, so I saunter up, sit beside him. He drapes an arm over my shoulders.

"Hey, Littlefoot."

"Hey, Sam." I poke his ribs, and he curves his body away from me.

"Want to be my date for the Walburg fair, Little One?"

"It's this weekend?"

"Yeah, Space-O. It starts tomorrow. Take a day off, come watch the chucks with me."

"Well, I should get back to the fire."

"Even the wicked deserve a break, Little Devil. Jen'll be out-riding."

"Okay, Sam-O, I will." I pinch his cheeks.

The next morning Will, Dad, and I saddle up. Will leaves Horse at home, opting for a bay gelding instead. Normally we'd give the calves a couple weeks to recover before moving them to new pasture, but these are strange days.

The cows are eager to get to the Elmhurst pasture, which is two miles down the road. I have to ride in front of them to slow them down, to keep them with their calves. They speed-walk the whole way, sometimes breaking into a trot, and turn into the pasture gate just past the Elmhurst cemetery.

By the time we finish, I'm exhausted from the heat. I have a quick shower, trying to get rid of the smoke that's soaked into my hair and skin. Fall into my unmade bed. The sheets stink like sweat, I think before I fall asleep.

# CHAPTER EIGHT

*I'm tied to the train tracks. I try to loosen the ropes, but I can't move. The ropes are so tight I can hardly breathe. The tracks press into my back and shoulders, shuddering as the train approaches. The vibration reverberates through my whole body.*

*Someone will save me. That's the way this story goes. A fragile young woman in a frilly dress lies helpless across the train tracks. She's tied to the tracks, but her dress is so heavy, her corset so tight, and her heels so high that the rope is hardly needed to keep her down.*

*But it's okay because a handsome young hero with a white hat and handlebar mustache will save her. He'll trick the villain, always easy to spot by his black hat and mustache, waxed and moulded to a fine point.*

*This hero will untie me and carry me away from the tracks, gently deposit me on my feet. I just need to cry out for help.*

*I scream and scream, but no one comes. The train whistle fills my ears, so loud that I can't hear myself scream anymore.*

My alarm wakes me up at five-thirty. I don't have any clean clothes. I sort through my semi-clean pile, then settle on a faded pair of blue jeans and a light, loose-fitting red shirt. I make a small coffee, mix in a little Bailey's, and just as I'm pouring it into a travel mug filled with ice, Sam pulls up.

Nitty Gritty Dirt Band is blaring from the after-market speaker system of Sam's half-ton. Sam's got his party mix playing, mostly rowdy country. Not a good sign.

I walk up. Sam is smoking a cigar and drinking from a mickey of Wiser's.

"Ready to party, Littlefoot!" It's not a question. More of a threat, I think.

"Want me to drive, Sam? I'm drinking coffee." I hold up my mug.

"No. Sit back and enjoy the ride!" I reluctantly climb into the passenger side.

Sam is a wild driver at the best of times, but even worse when he's drinking. He keeps his truck at somewhere between 120 and 130 kilometres an hour the whole way into Walburg, the back end of the truck constantly fishtailing on the rough gravel roads.

My anxiety grows as we get closer to the Englishman River. The coulee is so steep.

When we reach the Englishman River, he actually speeds up, whooping as we plummet toward the river. I brace my legs and close my eyes, imagining us plunging down the steep ditch, through the barb-wired fence, and settling upside down in the river. Just before the cab of the truck fills up with water, the engine will burst into flames. The medical examiner won't be able to tell if we burned to death or drowned.

"Open your eyes, Little Pussy," Sam yells, flicking my ear.

"Fuck you, Sam! Keep your hands on the wheel!" I should have gone back to the fire, I think. It's way safer.

"Yee-ha!" Sam drains the mickey and tosses it out the window.

Once he parks at the fairgrounds, I slap him, hard.

"Shit! What was that for, Littlefoot?"

"For almost killing us, you ass! I'm never letting you drive me anywhere again!" Fucking Sam. I storm ahead of him, and he has to trot to keep up.

We walk past the slow-pitch teams and start weaseling our way through the fair crowd. There're hundreds of people here eating cotton candy and hotdogs and drinking beer. We walk by a little boy giving his mom the play-by-play of the demolition derby from earlier in the day.

I feel something greasy on my big toe. Glance down at my flip-flops and realize I've stepped in a discarded, partially eaten cheeseburger.

Even though we're miles from Turtle Lake, the air is a blue-grey haze. I run my hands through my hair and realize it too stinks of burning trees and brush. The fire won't quite let us go, I think. It's everywhere.

There will be a dance tonight, and tomorrow night, too. The dance is usually exciting because people get a little tight, and then they get a little rowdy. But my favourite part of the fair has always been the chuckwagon races.

At St. Walburg, each heat includes three chucks — a team of four thoroughbreds pulling a chuckwagon and driver, and two outriders on horses. At the start of the race, one outrider holds the lead chuckwagon horse until the horn goes. Then the second outrider throws a barrel, or stove, into the back of the chuckwagon. The chuckwagon driver and outriders must all make a clean figure eight around the barrels before racing around the track. Outriders must finish within one hundred and fifty feet of their chuckwagon or the chuckwagon driver gets a one-second penalty.

Sam and I make our way around the track to the field where the chuckwagon people have their trailers. Since Jen started working for the Wrights, I've hung out with them a few times during the races. The chuckwagon circuit is a family affair, with sons riding as outriders for their fathers and other drivers, and everyone helping each other.

The first person I recognize is Maggie Wright, whose husband, Frank, has a team of chucks. She's helping her son-in-law, George Starchild, hitch up his horses. George was one of the first drivers to take Jen on. Maggie sees us coming, and her smile reaches her eyes. "Jen's saddling up," she says, nodding her head in the direction of the trailer.

Jen's saddling a tall, blood-bay mare. The mare must be seventeen hands.

The mare's left ear twitches toward me, and she nickers as we approach. Jen's about to embrace Sam, but she sniffs, stops.

"You're loaded!"

"Oh, no, I'm okay, Jenny." Big mistake. Sam only calls her Jenny after he's had a few drinks. Jen's nails are digging into the palms of her hands as she turns and faces me.

"Who drove?"

"Sam did," I say.

"I don't know who's stupider, him for driving or you for letting him."

"Believe me, I feel like an idiot," I say.

"Yeah, no kidding," Jen says. She laughs quietly to herself. Well, I'm not sure if I could even call it a laugh. It's more like a spasm. She pulls her cinch tight and loops the lead rope around the saddle horn. Then she leaps into the saddle. The mare jigs, chewing on the bit. They trot past us to the track.

"She's pissed at us," Sam says. I could slap him again, I'm so mad.

Maggie Wright invites us to stay, offers us lawn chairs and drinks.

"Darby, we're hoping you'll stay for the dance and sing a song or two with the band. We sure like the way you sing 'Folsom Prison Blues.' It's the only time I can get my man to dance with me."

"You're so sweet, Maggie."

"Now tell me about the fire. How are you all holding up out there?"

"Okay. Tired. It's sort of monotonous a lot of the time. Then something crazy happens, like a hotspot flares up, or someone gets hurt, or the wind changes. Fred Schmidt's Cat burnt up two days ago. That was exciting."

"Oh, no. That's sure bad news for Fred."

"Yeah. He wasn't real happy. But no one got hurt."

The thing about the fire is it doesn't seem like real life. I mean, obviously the fire is real, and it's a real problem. But while I'm there, I can forget about mundane things like work. And I can almost forget about the big things, too. Like my train-wrecked relationship with Luke. The bullshit the cops are spouting about Will. And the very slim chance that Steele's accusations aren't bullshit at all.

I can't even consider that one for long. I'd rather watch the whole forest burn than find out my uncle is a monster.

George almost wins his heat. He comes in first, but Jen has trouble getting on her horse at the beginning and finishes too far behind, incurring a penalty.

"That's strange. Jen never gets penalties like that," says Maggie. "Oh, she doesn't look happy about it either."

The mare trots past us, and Jen's face is twisted up like a gargoyle's.

"Littlefoot, you should've drove," says Sam.

I sigh. I'm getting very tired of Sam right now.

"I have to go to the bathroom," I say, getting up.

I head immediately to the bleachers to watch the next heat. Jen's in this one, too. She usually has nine or ten races a night. I want a spot high up on the bleachers, but they look full.

Someone at the top is waving at me. The sun is in my eyes, and I can't tell who it is. I start climbing anyway.

I'm almost at the top when I realize it's Jack. I stop, my foot in midair, my body tilting backwards slightly. But I have to keep going. It would be rude to turn around and leave. And people would notice, would wonder.

Dammit.

Jack's arm is still in a cast. One signature sprawls across the length of it. *TED ROGERS.*

"You don't have many friends out here, do you?" I joke as I

sit beside him.

"Just you and Ted." He looks at me sideways, and I blush, fix my eyes straight ahead.

"Well, I'm not signing your damned cast."

Will is at the bottom of the next set of bleachers, bidding on this heat's chucks. I guess he needed a break from the fire, too. We should all set up some sort of schedule, I think. Set up shifts, make sure everyone gets a day or so off every week.

Will wins the bid for the wagon Jen's riding with this time. There's a group of people standing around him, and they all laugh as he raises a fist, shouts, "Go get 'em, Jenny!"

This break is agreeing with him, I think. He looks better than he did even a day ago. His skin isn't tight and shiny and grey. And the cops haven't been hovering around him for a couple days now, either. That probably helps.

Jen is holding the lead horse of her chuckwagon team. The horn blares, and Jen leaps into the saddle as easily as a cat jumping onto a window sill. She follows her chuck around the barrels, and then her horse is tearing up the oval track, Jen leaning forward, close to the horse's neck. She catches up to her chuckwagon driver just before the last turn and has to pull her horse down to avoid a penalty. She does it, though. She makes a clean run, and so does the other outrider. This time her driver wins his heat.

Will's group bursts into whoops and hollers, celebrating his win.

After the last race is done, Jack asks me if I want a ride back home. I know I shouldn't. I'll end up in the back seat of his vehicle on a grid road, like some small-town virgin who doesn't know any better.

I really shouldn't.

With the fire still burning at Horseshoe Bay, Jack can't get back to his cabin, so he's borrowed a silver Airstream and camped at Brightsand Lake. He's in the group campsites, away from the main beach, in the east section of the park. His campsite is tucked into a large patch of black spruce trees, which make the site very private.

Jack fires up the barbeque, starts flipping burgers, all with one arm.

"Pretty good for a cripple," I say.

"You want a burger or not?

"Sure. It's really not the same without a campfire, though, is it?"

"No," Jack says. "But I'm not going to be the one to break the fire ban and burn down the park. I'll really be homeless then."

I load my burger with mozzarella, lettuce, tomatoes, pickles, and jalapeno peppers. Then add mustard, relish, and salsa. My burger is a shaky, mile-high monster that I can barely wrap my teeth around. The bottom half of the bun is soggy with condiments. The first bite smears sauce on my chin, but I don't care.

We sit on top of the wooden picnic table, munching our burgers. Jack passes me a piece of paper towel. I shake my head no, chewing quickly. Jack laughs.

"Give me a break," I mumble around a mouthful of burger. "I didn't have supper." A piece of cheese tumbles down my chin and into my cleavage.

"Obviously you're not too worried about impressing me anymore," Jack says, grinning.

"News flash, Jack. I was never worried about impressing you. Can I have another burger?"

"Please do. You look like you haven't eaten in weeks."

He nods toward the barbeque. I load up another burger, plop down beside him again on the picnic table. We chew in silence for a minute, and then I ask Jack how it feels to be the other man.

"Fine, just fine," he says.

"You don't feel guilty?" I ask.

"Of what? You're not married. You're not even in a serious relationship."

"What? Luke's serious! I've been with Luke for years," I say.

"Give me a break," Jack smirks. "You will never be serious about Luke."

"Maybe I will." I know I sound peevish, and this annoys me even more. "He asked me to move to Saskatoon with him this fall while he finishes school." I haven't told anyone else about this. Dad and Grandma Swank will freak.

When Grandma found out I was applying to MacEwan's music program, she helped me practise every night. She'd have me slide up an octave from the pitch she was playing, then an octave below. Then she'd play a pitch that was out of my range, and I'd have to match it within my range. I hadn't done those kinds of vocal exercises since high school, and it was tough for me at first. Grandma helped me stick it out, though.

When I mentioned that I needed to perform a jazz etude, Grandma called someone at the College and had them mail her a copy of the etude. She made me practise it over and over, probably a hundred times. I had to pick another piece to perform, and Grandma insisted that I find a jazz piece. She rejected all my suggestions until we finally settled on "Come Fly With Me." Grandma dug out her Frank Sinatra songbook, and I rehearsed until I was completely sick of Ol' Blue Eyes. Grandma even came with me to Edmonton so she could accompany me on the piano during my audition.

Jack is staring at me like I've grown a second head. "You can't be serious. Why would you even think about moving in with Luke?"

"I kinda feel like I should. I mean, he's a great guy, and he loves me ..." These are all lies, or partial lies. The truth is I'm scared. Scared that school will be too hard, that I won't make it as a musician. Scared that I won't find anyone as good as Luke.

"Fuck." Jack sets his burger on his plate, rubs his hand over his face.

"Why do you care? We both know this isn't long term."

"I don't even know what to say to you, Darby."

"Sure you do, Jack. Just go ahead, say it."

"Okay, well, to start with, you don't love him. I know you don't, you know you don't, everyone but Luke knows you don't."

"Oh, come on, maybe I do. Or I will. I could, maybe ..."

"No, you never will. Second, what about Edmonton? What about school?"

"I don't know ... Sometimes the whole music thing seems like a long shot. I talked to Luke about it, and I'm probably going to spend a bunch of money on tuition and end up back where I started. Waitressing."

Jack sighs, picks up a paper towel, and wipes the sauce from my face. "Darby, I can't tell you what to do. You're the only one who can make that kind of decision. Just make sure it's you who's making it."

"I just feel like I'm being pulled along sometimes, and it's easier to go with the flow than fight it. You know?" I kick off my flip-flops, stare at my dusty toes. "Can we talk about something else?"

"Sure. I spent the morning fishing at the trout pond. Caught nothing, but I guess I have an excuse." He waves his cast. "And you?"

"Oh, vaccinated calves. The last few weeks have been weird." And I tell him everything. I tell him about Will swearing at me a few days ago. Then I tell him about Steele's suspicions of Will, of how stupid I feel for not knowing about any of it. It all comes out in a gush, and when I finish, I inhale a lungful of smoky air. Feel lighter.

"Do you think he did it?"

"I don't know," I say. "I can't believe it. I can't believe anyone I know would do that to someone they love."

"I don't think it has anything to do with love," Jack says.

"What are you going to do?"

"What can I do? The cops want me to help, but I don't know anything. And even if I did, I don't know if I can tell them."

"How can you say that?" Jack says, anger at the edge of his voice. "Your aunt is dead. If your uncle did it, he deserves to rot in prison."

I try to think of the best way to explain why I can't betray my family to the cops. Somehow 'it's not their business' doesn't seem like enough.

"You grew up in a small town, Jack. You know what it's like. We're all the sum of our relationships."

"No, we're not, Darby."

"Yes, we are. If someone does something stupid, or gets sick, or hurt, everyone talks about that. And then they talk about how that person is related to someone else they know, and then how that second person is related to another family branch. And if you're giving someone directions, you don't say, 'Turn left at the green house.' You say, 'Turn left at the old McNab house.' And everyone still calls it the 'old McNab house' even though it's been twenty years since a McNab lived in it. Families, relationships, they literally mark our landscape out here."

"Okay, well, what's your point? You'd be too ashamed to have a murderer in your family?"

"Well, no. Or yes. But it's more than that. I mean, family is everything, right?"

"Bullshit, Darby. If it means protecting a murderer, family is nothing."

"What the hell do you know, Jack? You think you know what you'd do? I fucking doubt it. Things don't usually work out too well for the whistle blowers, you know."

"Okay, sorry. I don't want to fight with you," Jack says.

We sit in silence for a minute.

"This isn't the first time this kind of thing has happened around here, you know," I say. "I went to elementary school in

Livelong. You know the building that holds the post office and the bar? That used to be our school."

Jack says nothing. Waits.

I take a deep breath, continue.

"When I was in grade three, we had this new kid in our class. His name was Corbett. Corbett's real dad had died in a car accident, and his mom had moved in with this guy that lived across from the school. I don't remember his real name, but we always called him Pop for some reason. He had a round belly and a short white beard. He played Santa Claus at the school Christmas concerts. I always knew it was Pop, not Santa, but I never told anyone else because I thought it might hurt Pop's feelings for some reason.

"At lunch, Corbett always mooched food off the rest of us. We'd give him our snacks, or the stuff we didn't like. Whenever I had peanut butter sandwiches, I let Corbett have them. He'd eat anything. Then our teacher started bringing him lunches and there was no one to eat my peanut butter sandwiches.

"One morning Corbett wasn't at school. I didn't see him again. Our teacher said he and his mom moved to North Battleford, to be closer to his grandma. I didn't find out the truth for a long time. Sam's older sister, who was friends with Corbett's older sister, told me the rest of the story.

"Turns out Pop used to beat the hell out of Corbett's mom. And sometimes he hit Corbett and his sister too. Corbett would try to protect his mom and sister, and Pop would beat him, but always on the torso so no one would see the bruises. Can you imagine, a grade three kid trying to protect his family? Anyway, some people in town knew about it, but they didn't want to believe it, or they didn't know what to do. Pop was kind of charismatic — he always had a bunch of people hanging around him, listening to his bullshit stories. Most people really liked him.

"There was this one guy, Big Jake, who owned the Livelong Hotel. He was actually a little guy, but people called him big because he could toss troublemakers three times his size out of the bar like it was nothing. Which pissed a lot of people off. Some of his customers thought he was too rough.

"Anyway, Big Jake found out what Pop was up to, and he told him to stay the hell out of his bar. Right in front of a bunch of people. He said he wanted nothin' to do with a fuckin' wife-beatin' piece of shit like Pop. And then he said if Pop didn't stop beating the kid, he was going to call the goddamn cops. Pop was super pissed, but he left.

"That same night, after Big Jake had kicked out the last of the drunks, he was about to lock the door when Pop burst in. He punched Big Jake, laid him right out. Then he kicked him and basically beat the living hell out of him. He pulled out a filleting knife and tried to stab Big Jake, but Big Jake rolled away and managed to get on his feet.

"There was something about Big Jake that most people didn't know. He'd spent a few years in prison, in Prince Albert. I'm not sure what for. Sam's sister didn't really know. Some people say he killed a guy in a fight, some say he just beat the shit out of someone. Whatever he did to end up there, prison made Big Jake a tough man to beat.

"Anyway, before Pop even knew what was happening, Big Jake had clocked him with a chair. Pop dropped the filleting knife, and Big Jake got hold of it and stabbed Pop. Right in the heart.

"Right then some locals wandered in, hoping for a last drink, and saw Pop laying on the floor. A couple of them held Big Jake back, another called an ambulance, and Pop lived. Barely.

"The cops charged Big Jake with attempted murder, and most people in town blamed him. They didn't know the whole story, or didn't want to know. In the end, Big Jake got off, 'cause it was self-defense. And Corbett and his mom got away from Pop while he was in the hospital. I don't know what happened to them. I hope they were okay after that.

"But even after Big Jake got off, a lot of people didn't believe Big Jake's side of it, or just didn't want much to do with the whole thing. Business kinda dried up for him. If he'd stuck around, things might've got better for him, but he'd had enough. He sold the bar and left town."

Jack lit a smoke, took a drag. "So, what's your point? Big Jake survived. The bad guy ended up in the hospital. Corbett and his mom got away."

"Yeah, but Big Jake could've died. And everyone in town was pissed at him."

"So? You're not Big Jake. People aren't going to be mad at you."

"How do you know that? People like my uncle. And they don't want to admit that this happened in their neighbourhood."

"What about your aunt? She deserves justice, Darby."

"My aunt's dead. Justice won't bring her back. And I don't even know if Will did it. I don't want to believe he killed her." The tears begin.

"Darby, if you need anything, I'll help you."

"I know." I pull him to me, and kiss him slowly.

Later that night, I wake up in Jack's trailer. Put on my clothes and go outside for a smoke. The forest fire smell still hangs in the air, but the night sky is clear.

Perched on the picnic table, looking up at a starlit sky so beautiful it hurts, I think of Big Jake and Corbett's mom. I wish someone like Big Jake had been around for Aunt Bea. I wish someone had saved her.

# CHAPTER NINE

Slowly we begin to smother the flames, and by late July the Cherville farm is safe. The fire isn't exactly extinguished, but driven underground, smouldering deep in the muskeg. It might wait weeks, even months, to flare up. Still, we have won this battle. We celebrate.

Luke and I head to the Northlander bar that afternoon. We take one of the tables near the window, looking out on Turtle Lake. Local farmers, cabin owners, acreage owners, people from Thunderchild reserve, and a few government firefighters drift in that afternoon, needing to celebrate. We all swap firefighting stories. Two high school boys from the reserve say one of the firebombers dropped a payload of water and foam on them, knocking them flat to the ground. An older farmer says he and his buddy drove a truck right through the fire, which had crossed the dump road near Moonlight Bay. He says his whiskers were singed. Everyone at the table groans.

"Bullshit, Brad," another farmer yells when the story is finished.

"It's true," Brad cries. "Well, maybe not the part about my whiskers."

I decide to believe him.

A spontaneous leg-wrestling tournament breaks out. I beat Sam, Luke, Jen, Bill, and a couple of firefighters, but Janice, the waitress, knocks me out of the tournament. She goes on to win the whole thing.

"I knew I had it won after I beat that one," she says, pointing at me with her lips. We laugh.

By six o'clock, every table at the bar is full, and more people are coming through the door. Kid Rock blasts from the jukebox, and the dance floor is a mosh pit. The older people have commandeered tables near the back, while the rest of us cluster around the bar and on the dance floor. We all dance and jump and slam against each other, sweat and booze soaking our clothes.

Against all odds, a young firefighter from Meadow Lake talks Carrie, the bar manager, into setting up the karaoke machine. He's a stocky boy with a pudgy baby face and a rooster tail. And he's the worst singer I've ever heard. As he powers through 'Every Rose Has Its Thorn,' I can't stop grinding my teeth.

"Darby, please, for the love of God, get up there," Carrie begs. "I don't know what I was thinking, pulling out that thing."

"Can I dance on the bar?"

"Don't crack your head open. Please."

The crowd is packed tight around the karaoke machine, clawing for the microphone. I move through them like a salmon swimming upstream. A drunk girl, barely nineteen, clutches the mic, flipping through the catalogue. Unable to settle on a song.

"Here, honey, I'll take care of that," I say and snatch the mic from her sweaty fingers.

I pick 'We Are The Champions' because Freddie Mercury is my hero and the song is our victory cry. We are full of adrenalin and booze and life. No time for sissy power ballads or reflective folk songs or anything that's not pure, loud awesome. I climb onto the bar, gracefully, I imagine, despite the six or so beers I've already drunk.

The bar top is a fiery, bloody river, roiling across a black sky. Terrible and beautiful. Carrie had commissioned it from Bea a few years ago, but I'd grown so used to it, I'd stopped seeing it until now.

I am standing on Dante's Inferno, I realize. And my voice is a water bomber engine, roaring above the bar noise.

Cheers move through the bar like whitecaps. Another firefighter, this one cut like stone, asks if he can buy me a shot.

"You can buy me a rye," I say. I jump behind the bar, open my mouth, and Janice pours a shot of rye down my throat. The hot firefighter raises his drink and cheers.

"Put on some Motörhead," I cry.

The night becomes a blur of shots and hard-rock songs. Two more girls climb up on the bar. We all dance as we take turns singing. Well, if you could call it dancing. Sometimes the hot firefighter crawls up on the bar, singing with us. Carrie and Janice sling drinks around our legs.

As the night wears on, I scream as much as sing, my voice ripping through my throat. At one point, Luke appears, tugging on my leg, trying to pull me down from the bar.

"Darby, we should go," he says.

I shake my head no, and the hot firefighter pushes Luke away. After that, I lose track of him.

Much later, I'm standing by the window, watching the sun rise over Turtle Lake. The sun's tinted the lake blood-red. And then I see Bea. She's coming out of the water, fully clothed, soaking wet. Her eyes are black, and the water running off her is on fire.

I drop my beer.

"What's wrong?" Janice steers me away from the broken glass.

I look back out the window, but nothing's there.

"Nothing. Drank too much."

I wake up at seven o'clock, stretched out on the bench seat of my Jeep. My cell phone is vibrating on the dash, scuttling toward the edge. I grab it just before it falls.

"Darby, it's Jack."

I grunt.

"Listen, the restaurant is in one piece. I want to reopen

tomorrow for breakfast. I need you to help me clean up, get some fresh vegetables, all that stuff."

I moan. There is a sandstorm battering the walls of my throat, and my mouth tastes like a garbage dump. A car alarm goes off somewhere.

"Are you okay? Where are you?"

I slowly sit up, trying not to rip the skin from the right side of my face, which is stuck to the green vinyl seat. The truck is steaming hot, so I unroll a window.

"I'm at Northlander. Parking lot."

"Can you be here in an hour?"

I hang up. Open the driver's door and puke into the dusty gravel.

We open the Shoe at eight o'clock the day after my hangover. Locals stream in, stocking up on food from the store and filling the tables in the restaurant. Jack whistles as he cooks scrambled eggs, omelets, hashbrowns, bacon. His cast is off and he's fast. The tables fill up quickly, and all anyone can talk about is the fire. Horseshoe Bay was hit hard, and many people lost their cabins. Across the road, some of the houses on the reserve are gone, too. Hotspots linger. Bob Friendly, Ross Cherville, and three other men come in for breakfast. The other customers start firing questions at them right away.

"Think it'll flare up again?"

"You guys still watching for hotspots?"

"Government firefighters still here?"

Ross and the other men spit out answers between bites of egg and toast. I field questions about the bear, too. They haven't caught him. He's too smart for the live trap — even carcasses and rotten garbage can't tempt him into the metal cylinder.

"Nice fire you made there, Friendly," sneers Todd Manning.

Bob stares into his breakfast. I know he hasn't slept for days. I consider sloshing coffee into Todd's lap.

Becky shows up late, and I end up handling the lunch shift on my own. When she ambles in at one thirty, I feel like a long-tailed cat locked in a room full of rocking chairs.

"Nice timing," I snipe.

"Whatever."

"No, not 'whatever,' you little snot." I grab her elbow, pull her into the kitchen. "If you can't show up on time, you can find another job. And I won't give you a good reference, either."

Becky's mouth is an outraged O. She looks to Jack for back-up.

"Darby's the boss. And she's right," he says, then shrugs and goes back to flipping burgers.

"Fine. But you shouldn't throw rocks at glass," she sniffs.

I laugh, and she rolls her eyes.

"Just wash those dishes, Becky. We're almost out of cutlery."

It's steady all afternoon. People are itching to gather for coffee, talk about the fire. We run out of apple pie just before the supper rush. We run out of the special, pork ribs, by seven thirty. Things start to die down at nine, and I send Becky home while I take care of the stragglers.

We close the Shoe at ten, and by ten thirty Jack is locking the back door.

"Come over for a glass of wine."

I hesitate.

"Oh, come on, Darby. I won't bite."

"Okay."

Jack's cabin is two rows back from the lakefront. It's a true cabin — a modest, one-storey square. The deck in front is covered with that gross green outdoor carpet. But it's well maintained: the shingles are new and the gutters clean. The forest-green wood siding makes the cabin blend into the surrounding spruce. Cabin camouflage.

Someone has bought the lot to the left of Jack's, ripped down the Ducharmes' original A-frame. The new owners were in the Shoe this afternoon studying plans. The plans remind me of the houses we gawked at when we drove through Sherwood Park after my recital at MacEwan. They've cut down all the spruce, too, to make room for their retirement home.

Inside, Jack's cabin is divided into one kitchen/living room at the front. Three rooms, including one bathroom, are separated from the main room by curtains. No drywall or lino — everything is rough pine.

Jack opens a bottle of red, pours. Hands me the biggest wine glass I've seen. It looks like it could hold half a bottle.

"You're gonna love this," he says as he puts on a CD.

It's country. Good country. A man's voice, a tenor sometimes leaping into coyote yips. He strums frantically on the acoustic. Decent player, lots of energy. The first song begs his love to take him back, to blame him for everything if that's what it takes. I can relate.

"Jesus Christ, this is my theme song. Who the hell is this guy?"

"The long dead Handsome Ned. My older cousin was a sound guy at a bar on Queen Street West. We visited them one summer — I think I was sixteen — and Jay snuck me into the bar to see this guy. He blew me away. Jay taped the show, and he just sent me a CD a couple weeks ago — he said it was the fifteenth anniversary of the show. Great, hey?"

"Yeah. Wine's not bad either, Jack."

Jack pulls the glass from my hand.

"Let's dance."

He swings me around the floor as though he was born dancing. I had no idea he knew how to two-step. As we dance, I sing to Jack.

We dance through two songs. Then Handsome Ned speaks to me from the grave.

*There's something sad and lonely about a freight train slipping
on wet steel, rolling back to places I've been.*

*An old steam whistle keeps calling my name again and again.*

I feel small tremors, as though an earthquake is beginning.
Or a train's coming down the tracks.

"What's wrong?" Jack stops dancing.

"Fucking trains. If I never hear about or see a train again, I'll
die a happy woman."

"Don't take it so personally. I doubt Handsome Ned had you
in mind when he wrote 'Steel Rail Blue.'"

I shiver again.

"Darby, what's wrong?"

I pick up my glass of wine, fortify myself with a long drink.
Then I rant.

"Every night I dream about trains. I can't sleep more than
twenty minutes without seeing and hearing and feeling a train
coming toward me. I'm either tied to the tracks or being chased
by some horrible creature right into a train. Or I'm watching
my mom's old barrel horse run right into a train. That one's the
worst. Jesus fucking Christ, I'm sick of trains. Just the thought
of a train whistle makes me throw up in my mouth."

"Wait, Darby ... What did you say about the horse and train?"
Jack pulls me toward a laptop on the kitchen table. "What did
the horse look like?"

"It was my mom's mare. She was fast as hell. Thoroughbred–
quarter horse cross, muscular hindquarters. Black. Completely
black. And she always runs right along the tracks, right to the
train. She never gets off the tracks. And I can't do anything ...
What are you doing?"

Jack's logged in to his laptop and is opening up Firefox.

"I just got high-speed hooked up yesterday," he grins. "You
have to see this."

He Googles "Horse and Train."

And a still image from my dream pops up.

I drop my wine glass. Red wine splashes all over my legs and feet. I step back, right onto a shard of glass.

"Fucking hell!" Blood oozes from my heel.

I'm sitting under the large arborite table in Bea's studio, flipping through her art magazines and humming the song I always sing to Oliver, my Shetland pony. Oliver doesn't always listen to me. Sometimes when we're moving cows, he runs right through the herd. And he always follows Magic, no matter where Mom and Magic are going. But I still love him.

I sing "9 to 5" very softly, trying to mimic Dolly Parton's vibrato.

I love Dolly Parton. She's pretty, and she has a good voice. And she's smart. The bus driver always plays my Dolly Parton tape on the bus. The older boys make jokes about her that I don't understand. Maybe they're jealous because she's smarter than they are.

I flip the page. A painting of Herefords. I draw Oliver in front of them. His ears are pinned back and he's bucking at the Herefords.

There's lots of noise downstairs. Dishes breaking. Yelling, from Aunt Bea and Uncle Will. Another sound that I don't know. Like the sound I make when I pat my leg to call the dog to me, but louder.

Bea is crying now.

I don't like crying, so I sing a little louder. I flip the page, and that's when I see the picture. A black horse, just like Magic, running toward a train. I put down my grey crayon. Why is the horse running at the train? Will they crash? Won't the train kill the horse?

I think about the trains at Turtleford. The whistles are always D minor. I just learned what D minor was a few weeks ago, at my music lessons, and I knew right away it was the sound of the Turtleford trains.

The train whistles sound sad, but the sound is right for them. I like the Turtleford trains, but I don't like the train in the picture. What does its whistle sound like? Why doesn't the picture's train stop for the horse?

I'm still thinking about these questions when there's a new sound downstairs. My mom yelling. She can yell louder than anyone I know, way louder than Uncle Will and Aunt Bea. She's using words she never uses, words that Dad shouts at the cows when they kick him or step on him or run the wrong way.

Uncle Will is yelling back, but Mom screams right over top of him. Screaming hurts my ears. It sounds wrong. I practise my major scale, just like Grandma taught me.

"Do Re Me Fa So La Ti Do."

C major is my favourite.

Something else breaks. The patio door slides open, then shut. Uncle Will's truck coughs, then starts, and everything is really quiet for a long time. I go back to studying the horse picture.

My head is heavy, so I lay down. When I wake up, Mom's carrying me from the car to our house. It's dark outside. I close my eyes, sleep again.

"Don't move." Jack sets a chair behind me. "Sit."

I lift my feet, and he sweeps glass into a blue metal dust pan. Then he soaks up the wine with an old Oh Susanna T-shirt.

"Are you okay?"

"Fine." My voice is sharp as a knife edge. Jack ignores it.

Jack gently pulls the bloody wedge from my heel, drops it into the dust pan. Retrieves a first-aid kit from the kitchen cupboard.

"Now, this will sting." He pulls out a bottle of iodine.

"I'm a big girl. I can take it." *Cowboy up, Buttercup.*

Jack dabs iodine on my cut gently, as though his kindness

will dampen the bite. Then he smears liquid bandage over the cut and tapes a gauze square on top.

"All better." I ease myself out of the chair, gingerly put a little weight on the heel. "Where's my wine?"

"Darby, what's wrong?"

"I don't want to talk about it."

Jack hands me another glass of wine. He looks into my eyes, and his eyes are so worried I'm afraid I'll cry, so I stare at the floor.

Jack takes my wine away, sets it on the kitchen table. Tries to look me in the eye, then gives up. Holds my hands.

"Darby, you don't have to tell me anything. But you *can* tell me anything. You know that, right? And I won't tell anyone, and I'll do whatever you want me to do."

I look at him, and the tears burst. Jack holds me, and I mumble into his shoulder.

"What? What did you say?" He holds me far enough away that he can look into my face.

"He killed her. I know it now. Will killed my Aunt Bea."

∩

I don't know what my next move is with Will. Jack thinks I should tell the police about the memory, but they already know about the abuse.

I decide to wait. Wait and see. Weather the storm.

Jack wants me to play one night at the Shoe. I keep telling him I'll think about it, hoping he'll forget. But he asks me every day.

"Jack, why do you want me to play so bad?"

He looks surprised. "Because I want to hear you sing. Aren't you a musician?"

"Yeah, okay, I guess."

"Great. We'll do it next Saturday. I want to put up a few posters."

I take Saturday afternoon off. When I arrive at six, the restaurant is nearly full. The screen door is propped open so that the servers can zip out to the customers on the deck. The staff table, normally in the corner beside the coffee machine, has been moved. A tall bar stool and a small amp stand in the space. I tune my acoustic guitar, then plug it into the amp. Strum a few chords. It sounds good.

I don't want to be here, though. There's a chunk of metal sitting in my stomach. Becky smiles at me as she power walks into the kitchen, and the metal shifts in my gut. That sweet smile is poison, I know it.

Jack appears with a microphone, plugs it in.

"Ready for me to introduce you?" Jack asks. I nod.

"Excuse me, ladies and gentlemen. Tonight we have a special treat for you. To celebrate the end of the fire and the re-re-opening of the Horseshoe, our very own Darby Swank will be performing for us. Please welcome Darby!" Jack claps loudly, then touches the back of my neck. He shouldn't touch me like that, I think. Everyone will know, if they don't already.

Before I start I scan the room. Two tables away sit my dad, Will, and Grandma and Grandpa Swank. Dad looks terrible. So gaunt.

Will's looking nearly as good as he did before Bea died, though. The cut on his face, from the fallen poplar, has finally healed, and his skin isn't at all swollen and weird anymore. He's joking with the people at the table behind them. Grandma frowns at him, and he turns back around, sits up straight in his chair.

At the very back Luke, Sam, and Sam's younger cousin, Cheyenne, are eating burgers and fries. My music teacher, Mrs. Shevchenko, and her family sit at the table next to them. Mrs. Shevchenko's hair is white now and cut into a blunt bob. Very stylish. A bright-red scarf winds around her neck. I don't know how she can wear a scarf in this heat, but she looks cool and sophisticated.

I start off with a Joni Mitchell song, swing into "Le Partisan," the English version, with barely a pause. I close my eyes and see a grey landscape, with French resistance fighters, dressed in grey. And suddenly I see Bea, in worn blue jeans and a grey sweater, saddling a bay colt. She turns and looks at me, and her eyes are hard, black rocks.

I decide to play the song that I started writing after Bea's last installation. I've played it only a couple times, but I can hear it in my head.

"This next song is for Mrs. Shevchenko. She's always encouraged me to write my own songs. This one's called 'Not the Girl.'"

Mrs. Shevchenko smiles, claps her hands in delight. Her husband, sitting across from her, gently takes her hands. They sit like that through the whole song, holding hands on top of the table.

*We float at the edge of night, shut out from the web of stars.*
*The dark sky reflects our pain.*
*I wish I could start all over again.*
*I'm not the girl you think I am.*

*I've sat here all day watching whitecaps beating at the beach.*
*I crashed into you, trying to sink my fears.*
*But I know we'll only drown our dreams in tears.*
*I'm not the girl you think I am.*

As I perform, Becky and the new server, a high school boy, take orders and bring out plates of burgers, fries, salads, steaks, baked potatoes. The boy, whose name I can't remember, has a worried look on his face and stutters slightly. Becky is laughing and confident as she slides discs of food on the tables. She winks at me as she whips by on her way into the kitchen. The long skirt of her blue dress trails behind her like a tail. I almost miss a note.

Becky comes back with four cans of Coke and tall glasses and walks to Luke's table. As she sets the drinks on the table, she leans over Luke and whispers something. I swear I hear the word *skank*. Then she looks over her shoulder at me. Luke stops chewing and sets his fork beside his plate. I do miss a note this time, and Mrs. Shevchenko frowns briefly, then smiles reassuringly at me.

> *You have soil in your blood, and I'm made of air.*
> *I've known for a long time we won't go anywhere.*
> *I never wanted to hurt you, I swear.*
> *But I'm not the girl you think I am.*
> *Not the girl you think I am.*

Everyone is clapping. Will actually stands up, and the rest of my family, then the rest of the restaurant, follow suit.

Luke stands, too, clapping slowly. He's staring at me as though I've stabbed a fork in his chest.

I hang my guitar on the stand, thank my audience, and practically run out the back door for a smoke break. As I light my smoke, the screen door yawns, and Luke grabs my arm, pulling me toward him.

"Are you cheating on me?"

I drop my smoke, quickly stamp it out before it catches on the scruffy grass. Say nothing.

"Are you cheating on me?" he asks again, his voice breaking a little.

"Who told you that? Becky? She's full of shit."

"Answer the question."

Shit. I'm so screwed.

"Yes. I cheated on you."

"With Jack."

"Yes."

"Why? Why would you do that to me again?" Luke pinches the bridge of his nose, as though I've given him a nose bleed.

"I don't know. Luke, I'm so sorry..."

Luke grabs my hands, looks at me so intensely I can't meet his eyes.

"It'll be okay. We'll work through it. I love you. I still want you to come with me to Saskatoon this fall. It'll be okay."

"I can't."

"What?"

I pull my hands away, step backwards.

"I'm not going to Saskatoon with you. I'm going to Edmonton."

"Darby, please. Come with me. I love you. We can fix it. I'll do anything you want. Maybe I can even take a couple years off, if you want to go to Edmonton for school."

Holy fuck. I can't believe he's saying this. I suddenly see the damage I've done to him. It's carved into his face.

I take his hand, gently. I force myself to look into his eyes.

"I don't love you, Luke."

Luke's mouth opens and closes, like a gasping fish. Then he turns and walks around the restaurant, toward the parking lot.

"Luke, I'm sorry," I call.

"Fuck you, Darby!"

At this exact moment, my entire family walks through the back door, looking to congratulate me.

"Oh, my," says my grandma. "Was that the Cherville boy?"

"Yes, Grandma," I say.

"Why would he swear like that?" Grandma asks. "I always thought he was a nice boy."

"I just broke up with him."

"Oh, Darby, why would you go and do something like that?" she clucks. "He was so good for you."

"Mom, stay out of it," says my dad. "Darby can make her own decisions."

Before she can open her mouth again, Grandpa pulls Grandma back into the kitchen, and they argue quietly. Grandma would change her tune if she knew Luke didn't want me to go to Grant MacEwan College, but I don't really care anymore.

"Probably the right decision," says Will. "Better now than later."

"Thanks," I mumble. I can't even look at him right now.

I glance at my watch. "I should get back in there. The show must go on."

Jen is gone, too, when I strap on my guitar. Sam's cousin Cheyenne stares at me, and Sam kicks her under the table.

I decide to start off the second set with "Deep Red Bells," a new song by Neko Case. After the confrontation with Luke I want to pour myself into a dark song.

As I start to sing, people stop talking, then stop eating. They are wrapped up in the eerie lyrics and sound of the song. When I hit the chorus the room seems to shift, as though shadows have replaced the light.

Partway through the song Will stands up and stares at me. His lip is pulled into a snarl, like a dog about to fight over a scrap of meat.

*Does your soul cast about like an old paper bag*
*past empty lots and early graves?*

The screen door slams shut behind him. I feel it shudder from across the room. People stare after Will. Mrs. Shevchenko shivers and pulls on her sweater.

I want to pick up the energy so I kick into Handsome Ned's "Put the Blame on Me," which I've been practising all week. I even yip like a coyote, and the crowd hoots and hollers in response. The rest of the set is high energy, and I'm actually sweating by the time I finish.

"Let's hear it for the immensely talented Darby Swank!" Jack looks at me, and for a moment I'm afraid he's going to kiss me in front of everyone, but he settles for slapping me on the back, like a football player or something.

Everyone stands, clapping and whooping. Mrs. Shevchenko actually stands on her chair, sticks her fingers in her mouth, and blasts a whistle that hurts my ears. Grandma Swank glances at her disapprovingly, but even she's abandoned her golf-course clap.

Dad looks proud.

After I've finished my last song, Dad asks me for a ride home.

We're silent for most of the drive. I want to pump him for information about Will, but I don't dare. I don't know what Dad will do, and I don't want Will to suspect anything.

I'm sure now that Will abused Bea. The broken bones, always blamed on a horse, seem like such obvious signs of abuse now that I feel stupid for missing them.

God, she even stayed overnight at the Turtleford hospital at least twice that I know of, now that I really think of it. Concussions. The first time I was little, just starting school, but I remember visiting her in the hospital.

I made her a card. On the front, I drew the whole family. Me and Mom and Dad and Will, of course. Inside I wrote, "Get well. We love you."

And when Bea read it, she cried, and Mom made me go sit in the hallway while she talked to Bea.

How could Bea stand it? And if Will finally killed her, why after all these years?

The biggest question of all: why didn't Mom and Dad ever

tell me about any of this? Why would my family hide it from me?

I don't know my family at all. They are strangers to me.

# CHAPTER TEN

The summer drags on. The water levels in the lakes drop lower and lower. Across the road from the Horseshoe, charred toothpicks of trees reach toward the sky.

Nature has turned on us. Drought, fire, rogue bear. Even the grasshoppers are like a biblical plague. I can't walk through the pasture without clouds of hoppers rising from the grass and engulfing me like smoke. The worst thing is that with so many of them laying eggs, the hoppers will be just as bad, or worse, next summer.

Every night I have nightmares now. Usually with the horse and train, but sometimes a variation. Something bad is going to happen to me, I'm sure of it.

I spend more and more time with Jack. We work long hours together, cooking, planning the week's specials, going through the books. Each night, after closing the restaurant, we go to his cabin, open a bottle of wine, and watch the moon rise over the lake. I have moved my toothbrush, makeup, clothes to his cabin.

When I do go home, Dad jokes about me being a stranger. I roll my eyes. I know he misses me, but I'm angry that no one ever bothered to tell me that my family's fucked up. I'm not brave enough to confront him, though, so I resort to passive-aggressive avoidance. It makes me feel ugly.

But I also pity Dad because he's so thin he looks as though he's being eaten alive from the inside by some sort of parasite or something. And his hair is turning white.

Wilson's moved in, though, and Dad lets the old dog sleep in the house. Feeds him steak and hamburger and expensive dog food, trying to fatten him up. The dog's still thin, but he's regained enough joy to tree Fluffy on a regular basis, so I guess Dad's doing something right.

Grandma and Grandpa Swank are over there a lot, too. But I never see Will over there anymore, or vice versa. They used to be at each other's places constantly, discussing everything, but not now, I don't think. In fact, Grandpa asks me one day if Dad and Will "have had a falling out."

"I really don't know, Grandpa."

Grandpa doesn't believe me, but I see no reason to fill him in on everything at this point. I wonder if he and Grandma have any idea what was going on. They must have. But then, I should have, too, but somehow I didn't.

Jen and Luke never come into the restaurant anymore. I haven't seen them since I broke up with Luke. This wears at me, pulls my spine into a question mark, makes me grind my teeth at night. My teeth grinding wakes Jack up, and then he wakes me up.

"What's wrong?" he asks one August night.

"I feel guilty about what I did to Luke."

"Maybe you should apologize to him."

"Oh, yeah, what about you? Don't you feel guilty?"

"I didn't screw him."

"You're awful, you know that?"

The next day is my day off. I need a break from the lake, so I go back to the farm for the day.

Dad isn't around. I go to my old bedroom, looking for a couple of CDs. Under my bed I find boxes of books and school projects from elementary school in Livelong. An illustrated story I created in grade four. Two Dr. Seuss books I never returned to the bookmobile. A stack of homemade valentines my friends gave me when I was in grade three. One is from Jen. It's a heart, with a frilly pink picture frame drawn around the edges. Inside the frame are two girls skipping rope, one with yellow hair, one with black hair. Underneath the picture is a rhyme we used to chant while skipping. I think Jen's dad taught it to us.

*Ripsaw, bucksaw, zipsaw, bang!*
*We are the Livelong school gang!*
*The boys are handsome,*
*The girls are sweet,*
*Livelong, Livelong, can't be beat!*

I flip the silly valentine over, not wanting to think about Jen. But right underneath Jen's valentine is one from Luke. It's a square piece of white paper, with blue sparkles stuck to the corners. In the middle is a large heart, filled in neatly with blue pencil crayon. Underneath the heart he's used a rainbow of pencil crayons to write *I give you my heart.*

I decide I need to say I'm sorry. Not the automatic *I'm sorry* people sprinkle through tough conversations when they're trying to deflect the other person's anger. Not the weak *sorry* that limped out of my mouth as I was breaking up with him. I wasn't sorry for breaking up with Luke, and I'm still not. But I am sorry for jerking him around.

I doubt Luke will listen to me for more than five seconds, so I write him a note, slip it into a large brown envelope, and print his name on the envelope. Then, at the last minute, I tuck his valentine into the envelope, too. I don't know why, but it feels like the right thing to do.

I try to imagine Luke reading my letter. Try to imagine the expression on his face. He'll still be angry, but maybe by the time he gets to the end, he'll be less hurt. I can see him moving his fingers down the page every time he finishes a line. Even though he's a good reader, he always does this when he's reading something important.

*Luke,*

*I wanted to tell you how sorry I am for hurting you. I shouldn't have lied to you for so long. You're so sweet and handsome and smart, and I convinced myself that I deserved someone like you.*

*But the life you're building is not what I want. When you're done university, you'll be ready to settle down into a good job. You'll probably buy a house and get married and start having kids. I'll spend my twenties becoming a musician (and waitressing). Once I'm done school, I'll be on the road all the time and playing in bars late at night. I'll be broke all the time, but I don't care.*

*I knew I couldn't do what you wanted. I should have told you sooner. I'm so, so sorry for that, because you deserve better.*

*I hope the next girl is more careful with your heart.*

*— Darby*

The spruce trees on the east side of the Chervilles' driveway are skeletons, their needles and branches incinerated. As I pull into the driveway, I stare for a moment at the black trees forming a horseshoe around the house, remembering the day we pushed the flames back from the yard. I thought the house was lost, but then the water bomber came, dropping frothy water on the house and trees. It was like a miracle.

Today the yard looks sad and burnt. There is nothing green here. I walk up to the front door slowly, puffs of dust rising with each step and sticking to my sweaty toes. Just as I'm about to knock, the door swings open, and Lena smiles at me.

"Darby, come in! The kids aren't home, but come in anyway. Do you want a coffee?" I hesitate, but Lena literally grabs my arm and pulls me through the door.

Looking at Lena, I can see exactly what Jen will look like in twenty-five years. Still beautiful, even with the lines around the mouth and eyes. They make her look softer, I think. But Lena can be a lion when she needs to. Mom always said Lena was a great nurse because if she knew a patient needed more care or extra tests, she would fight for them. She does the same for her kids.

I hope I'm not on her shit list right now.

"I just came to drop something off for Luke," I say as she ushers me into the kitchen. She takes the brown envelope from me, starts to open it, realizes it's sealed, and sets it on the kitchen counter. I know Lena and Jen too well — they're both snoopy as hell. She'll probably steam it open after I leave.

I sit at the table, and Lena pours me a cup of coffee. She sits on a tall stool and faces me, towering above me like a priest eyeing a sinner.

"Now, let me be clear, Darby. I don't like the way you treated my son. Ross keeps telling me that Luke's an adult and that he can handle himself. But I'm still his mother. And I think he's too kind-hearted for his own good."

I take a sip of coffee, trying not to look terrified.

"But your mom and your aunt were my best friends. So I'd like to hear your side of it before I decide."

Hear my side of it before she decides what, I wonder. Before she decides to excommunicate me from the neighbourhood?

"Well, I came to apologize to Luke for how I treated him. I should have been honest with him. I'm sorry it ended that way — I should have broken up with him earlier. I was afraid of hurting him."

Lena gives me a hard look. Then she sighs.

"You can't go through life letting your fear stop you from doing what you know is right, Darby." She stands up, moves to a shorter chair closer to me, and rubs my hand, and I know I've been absolved. "You know, some days I can't decide whether you look more like your mom or your Aunt Bea. When I became friends with your mom, I thought we'd still be gossiping around this kitchen table as old ladies. We joked about moving into the Lodge together so we could still do coffee."

But not Bea, I think. Lena doesn't say it, but I think she knew Bea wouldn't make it to old age.

Lena stirs her coffee slowly, the metal teaspoon rattling against the sides of the cup. I think about my mom and Bea, both gone now. I feel like I've been cheated.

Mom's death was bad enough. But I can't even think about how Bea died. How afraid she must have been. It makes me so angry that my pulse pounds in my head.

Lena is still stirring her coffee even though the sugar has long since dissolved. I think about all the times my mom and my aunt sat around this table with her, sharing secrets and drinking coffee. Just like we're doing now. I'm sure Lena knew everything. She was never afraid to ask a question, and she could keep a secret. I wonder if she'll share their secrets with me now.

"Lena, how did you become friends with my mom? Did you meet in nursing school?"

"Oh no, I was already working when your mom was in school. I actually got her a job at the Turtleford hospital. She was working in St. Walburg at first."

"So, how did you meet?"

"Well, I knew her from the neighbourhood, but I got to be friends with your mom through Bea."

"Did you meet Bea at a dance or something?"

"No, I didn't." Lena stops stirring her coffee, taps the spoon against the rim to shake off the extra liquid, and lays it gently on the table.

"Darby, I met Bea working at the hospital. Your uncle had beaten her senseless. He nearly killed her."

Lena tells me the whole story. It was a quiet summer evening, just after supper, when a man came in carrying a woman wrapped in a crazy quilt. It was my dad and Bea.

Bea was in rough shape. She was shivering and naked except for the quilt. She had a bad concussion, her eyes were black, and she was hyperventilating.

Once they started treating Bea, they found out that her left eardrum had burst, and Lena suspected she'd been raped as well. She'd also been choked with some sort of rope or cord. The doctor was horrified. He kept saying, "Who would do this to another human being?" over and over.

Dad stuck around to see how Bea was doing. Once Bea was stabilized, Lena pulled him aside to find out what happened.

Dad had dropped by to see if he could borrow Will's stock trailer. He knocked on the patio door, but no one answered. But he thought he saw someone inside, so he walked in.

Will was on the living room floor, straddling Bea and strangling her with a lamp cord. Dad hauled Will off her and pushed him away. Will came after him, so Dad hit him, hard. Then he wrapped Bea in a blanket and drove her to the hospital.

"Your aunt would have died if your father hadn't walked in," says Lena. "As it was, she was in the hospital for several days."

Lena tried to get Bea to call the cops, but Bea was reluctant. She didn't think the cops would be able to protect her, and she didn't want everyone to know about the abuse. So Lena suggested she leave Will and move back in with her family.

"What she said to me still makes my blood run cold," says Lena. "She said, 'Will told me he would kill me and my whole family if I left him.'"

I drop my coffee cup. Lena doesn't even stop talking as she walks to the sink to get a dishrag. "It was different then. The police couldn't do anything if she didn't want to file charges. So we couldn't do anything."

On the day Bea was released, Will picked her up from the hospital. He brought her flowers and helped her out to the truck. He even tried to charm the doctor, but the doctor refused to shake his hand. "I gave that doctor hell later," says Lena. "I told him he'd make things worse for her, acting so righteous."

After that, Lena checked in on Bea regularly, and they became good friends. Mom and Dad tried to help too. "Roy always knew when Will was in a mean mood. He'd help Will out with chores, and if Will was drinking, Roy would drink with him and keep him away from home until he sobered up. They'd drive around the backroads, throwing beer bottles at signs all night, then pass out at Roy's farm. Of course, Will still beat Bea. He just got smarter about it."

"Lena, do you know if Bea was leaving?"

"I'm sure she was."

"Did you give her the money?"

"Yes. I talked Ross into selling a quarter last year."

Lena is so matter-of-fact, as though everyone knows this. As though it's obvious. I'm not sure what to say.

"Where was she going?" I finally ask.

"I don't know. She wouldn't tell me. She said she'd contact me once it was safe for her."

"Did you tell the cops all this?"

"No, Darby. They already know about the abuse. They have the hospital records. If they don't have enough evidence to charge him already, what I know isn't going to help."

"How do you know that? Maybe this is the last piece they need to hit him with a murder charge." I stand up, stare down at her.

Cowboy up, I think.

But Lena won't budge. She takes a slow sip of coffee, then looks at me.

"This isn't the first time she tried to leave, you know. You remember when you were in grade twelve, when Will picked you up from school and took you to Saskatoon to meet Bea?"

Bea had met us at Lawson Heights mall, then took me shopping. I had thought the whole thing was strange. The impulsiveness of the trip. The cell phone calls on the way into the city, the way Will left abruptly afterward. How Bea started at every sharp sound while we shopped. But I didn't want to look a gift horse in the mouth.

"Bea's gone. I can't bring her back, Darby. I have to think of myself, of my family now. You do what you have to do, but be careful."

As I drive away, I think about the monster that lives across the road. How could I have grown up so close to someone so dangerous and not known it?

It's a lot harder to believe in monsters, to condemn them, when you know and like them. Even love them.

But if I can't condemn him, does that make me some kind of monster too? Or just a coward?

When my heifer won Grand Champion in 4-H, Uncle Will was the first to congratulate me, the first to shake my hand. And he bought the heifer back from me, and she's still part of his purebred herd. "One of my best cows," he still tells me sometimes.

When he found out I'd been accepted into Grant MacEwan College, he told me he and Bea had set aside a little bit of money to help me. "Five thousand. It won't cover everything, but it should help you put groceries on the table," he said. My Uncle Will, he's a generous man. Everyone's always said so.

And he always bought Bea flowers and made her tea when she was sick. And now I know that was his way of apologizing to her for making her sick in the first place.

I realize I haven't set foot in their house since the day Jen and I dropped off the casseroles. Just been through the yard, after vaccinating cattle. Bea's garden was dead by then. Skeletal tomato plants, shrivelled lettuce, brown potato plants barely visible through the chickweed and pigweed and quack grass.

And I wonder if he's still trying to make it all up to her somehow. If he's built a shrine in their house, placed her ashes on a pedestal in the living room.

Or maybe it's the opposite. Maybe now that she's finally out of his reach, he resents her even more. Maybe he's ripped down her art and left her urn on top of the fridge, surrounded by junk, teetering on the fridge's edge.

I can't reconcile the uncle I've known with the monster that's been revealed.

I don't know if I should be sad for everything my family's lost, or angry because of what he's taken, or afraid of what he might do.

# CHAPTER ELEVEN

I wish I was at the beach today. It's a perfect August day for stretching out on the sand, soaking up the heat, then plunging into the cool lake. Instead, I'm sitting on a thousand pounds of sweating horseflesh, swatting at the horse flies and grasshoppers flocking around us.

Dad, Will, and I are trying to move Dad's cows to the home pasture. The Elmhurst pasture has run out of grass already, and Dad has enough pasture at home to last for a couple weeks. Then he'll have to start feeding hay.

"God knows where I'll find hay this year," he'd grumbled as he explained the situation to me. "This whole goddamned country's in a drought. I should just sell them, if anyone's stupid enough to buy cows this year."

Dad has never talked about selling his cows before. It really worries me. I feel guilty for spending so much time with Jack.

I hadn't seen Will since he stormed out of the Horseshoe after hearing me sing the Neko Case song. I was sure he was guilty, and I was terrified of him.

But I was also sure that he had no idea that I knew what he'd done. His outburst at the Horseshoe was triggered by the song and his own guilt, not by suspicion of me, I thought. And that morning he greeted me warmly, like old days.

"How are you?" he asked.

"Good," I replied, trying to sound casual.

Will greeted Dad, but Dad's only reply was a terse nod, and

Will's smile vanished. Once we got to the Elmhurst pasture, Will went west looking for cattle, and Dad and I headed north.

I don't want to be here, but Dad needs my help. I couldn't say no. Besides, Dad will be with me the whole time.

The morning wears on, hotter and hotter. A few clouds have gathered overhead, but they don't amount to much. The cows don't want to leave the cool bush, and they're spread out over two quarters. That's 320 acres of bush and pasture to search. Dad and I keep gathering up small groups of cows and calves and moving them into a pen near the road, just past the Elmhurst cemetery. Will brings in a group of ten from the west. He thinks there are at least ten more, so he disappears again.

Once we have them all gathered in the pen, we're going to open the gate and push them north up the road until we reach Dad's home pasture. That's the plan, anyway. But every time Dad and I have a small group headed in the right direction, they suddenly break from the path and scatter into the bush.

The number of cows and calves in the pen slowly grows. It's early afternoon, and we're hurrying now, because the air is so heavy and the clouds are so dark that it might actually storm.

Dad and I have just pushed a group of ten cow–calf pairs into the pens. Will's brought another eight pairs, and they're talking about where else they should be looking. I start back along the trail that winds through the bush behind the cemetery and toward the spring-fed pond, as I think there might be a few more cows there. I hear a cow bawling the way cows bawl when they've lost their calves. A guttural, desperate call. Bucky balks, and I urge him forward, following the sound despite the unease in my stomach.

More cows are bawling now. We climb a small hill, and suddenly I see them. A group of three cows in the clearing around the pond. Two have black calves at their side. The cows lower and shake their heads, then raise them back up to bawl. I turn my gaze to the edge of the clearing. Bucky jumps to the side just as I see the bear.

A black bear. It's big, but thin. And it's dragging something into the bush.

The calf-less cow suddenly runs at the bear, head down, making a sound more like a roar than a moo. Before she reaches the bear, Bucky panics, twirls on his hind legs, flees.

Bucky runs full out down the trail, back to the corrals, and I lean far over his neck. We round a turn and nearly slam into Dad and Booter. I manage to pull Bucky down a short way down the trail.

"Where's the fire, Darby?" Dad says, chuckling at his terrible pun.

"Dad ... the bear ..." I'm so short of breath that I can't finish, but Dad knows right away. His whole face turns hard as ice.

"Where?"

I lead him back to the pond. The bear is gone now, but the cows are still there, huddled together. One cow has a slashed face. A blood trail leads into the bush.

"Fucking cocksucker!" Dad dismounts from Booter, who prances nervously. Bucky is blowing hard, his head high and ears pointed forward stiffly.

"Easy," I say to Bucky, trying to calm him. My voice sounds higher than normal.

"I've got to find that bear," Dad says. "Darby, you and Will get the last of the cows in and move them back home." He mounts up, tries to heel Booter forward. She balks.

"Dad, wait," I cry, horrified at the thought of being left alone with Will. "You don't have a gun. What are you going to do when you find the bear?"

"Shit." Dad thinks for a moment. "What's Sam's cell number?"

"5891. You're going now? You know that's insane, right? Let's finish moving cows first. Then you and Sam can track the bear."

"No. It'll be long gone by then."

There's no use arguing with him, I realize. Not with two calves dead and a chance to put a stop to it. "Okay." Dad digs his cell out of his jacket pocket, checks for service. Punches in Sam's number despite his nervous mare. He pauses before he completes the call. "You've got your phone, in case anything happens?"

"Yeah."

"Good."

He nods at me, then rides away.

I hear him talking to Sam as he rides after the bear. Booter is blowing air from her nostrils and keeps stopping and whirling away from the blood trail. Finally Dad dismounts again and leads her into the bush.

My heart is pounding in my ears, and I hear only fragments of the conversation.

"Dragged the calf away ... Yes, I'm sure, Darby saw it ... I'll meet you at the edge of the Elmhurst quarter ... Bring your hunting rifle."

I watch him leave, turning Bucky in a tight circle to keep him from bolting. I want to follow Dad, but I can't come up with a good reason. There are only a few pairs left to gather anyway. It won't take that long, I tell myself. And besides, Will has no reason to hurt me. I'm no threat. As soon as I see Will, I'll tell him about the bear. We'll move the cows down the road, back to Dad's home pasture, and that'll be the end of it.

Bucky and I circle around the three cows and start pushing them toward the road. The beat-up cow keeps turning around and bawling for her calf. I wave my arms and yell at her in frustration, but finally the damned cow swerves off the trail, barrelling into the bush back toward the spot her calf disappeared. I turn Bucky after her, and he accelerates from a walk to a gallop so fast that I don't have time to pull him down before we're in the bush.

Bucky is racing after the cow, jumping over the deadfall, and I'm pulling hard on the reins when he trips. I feel myself tumbling, in slow motion, over the saddle horn as Bucky falls to his knees. I slam into the deadfall and rocks and drought-hardened ground. For a second, pain flashes from my head down. Then nothing.

"Darby ... Darby ... Wake up, Darby."

My face is wet. My head feels like it's been stuffed full of burning cotton. Something is digging into my left hip. Maybe a rock. I must be lying on a rock.

"Darby, can you hear me?"

It sounds like Will. Something is dripping onto my face. He's pouring water on me. I open my eyes, and they explode with white-hot light. Will is a shadow crouching beside me. I close them again.

"Darby, open your eyes. Wake up."

Slowly, slowly, I open my eyes. Just a crack at first, then a squint, then all the way. The light still hurts, but slowly the pain in my eyes fades. My head is another story. Pain smoulders at the base of my skull, sending flames along the crown of my head to my face.

"Can you sit up a little, Darby?" I prop myself up on my elbows. Something is jabbing my left elbow. I pick up a piece of plastic, realize it's a piece of my cell phone. Shattered from the fall.

"Here, have some water." He passes me a water bottle, and I

take big gulps. Will smiles, and the skin at the corners of his eyes crinkles. He's wearing a long-sleeved plaid shirt. The top button is missing, looks like it's been ripped out. Probably snagged it on a branch. He must be burning up in that shirt, it's so bloody hot.

"You must have hit the ground hard, Darby. I didn't know if you were going to wake up there. Sure was worried. You just rest a minute, then we'll get you to the hospital somehow. You probably got a concussion."

"My horse?"

"Oh, that bugger is fine. See?" He points to his left, where Bucky and Horse are nibbling on brown grass. There are strips of hair missing from each of Bucky's front legs, and a tiny bit of blood, but otherwise he looks fine. In fact, he looks beautiful. It must be the way the light is coming through the clouds because his coat glows like the blade of a sword in a forge.

The voice of Grandma Swank's pastor echoes in my head. Something about the second seal, a fiery red horse.

*Its rider was given power to take peace ...*

It must be my head injury, causing my brain to spit out bits of Revelations like half-digested supper.

Will stands up. "Try to stand up, Darby. You'll have to walk a little, just to the road. Can you stand up?"

"I think so."

"Here, take my hand." Will bends forward a little, reaching for me with his left hand. I take it, start to pull myself up, when a gold ring, strung on a piece of string, falls from under his shirt and dangles in front of me.

Bea's missing wedding band. He's been wearing it around his neck all this time.

For a split second, I hesitate. I think of the bear.

Then I see Bea floating in the lake, her ring finger severed from her hand, and something inside me turns to steel.

*... and to make men slay each other.*

Will is still pulling me to my feet as I reach for the simple gold band. I pull hard on the string, break it. I am standing now. I look at Will. He doesn't move.

I slowly uncurl my fingers, look closely at the ring. Read the inscription out loud. "To Bea, my wife. Love, Will." I slide the band onto my ring finger. "Why?"

Will's face closes up. His eyes narrow, and his mouth becomes a crack in a concrete sidewalk. He pushes me hard, and I fall back to the ground. He pounces on me, holding me down, breathing hard in my face. I can smell his body odour and the sweat of his horse. For a moment I think he's going to rape me. I try to push him off me, but he wraps his fingers around my throat and laughs. It's a low, rumbling laugh. Thunder.

"Now you've done it, you nosy little bitch." His voice, a dark hole, swallows everything around us. "You've really fucking done it."

He is throttling me. My breath is disappearing. Dissipating into the dark sky. I tuck my chin against my neck, trying to protect my throat. Futile. I panic, thrash hard, punch his chest, twist my body, trying to unseat him. Jackfish fighting on the line. Claw at his hands, then dig my fingernails into his face until they are red. He spits in my face, hits me hard, and my jaw throbs.

But he's let go, and the air rushes down my throat, fills my lungs. I start to crabwalk backwards, away from him. He grabs my throat with his left hand, squeezing hard, and raises his right for another jumbo strike. I squeeze my eyes shut. The clouds murmur with thunder. My left cheekbone takes the blow, and I wonder if it's broken. It hurts, but in a distant way, as though it's happening to someone else. Black dots swim at the edge of my eyes, multiplying, moving toward the centre. I think of my dad, of how sad he'll be that this happened when he was so close. Almost close enough to save me, if he knew.

Far away, I hear a squeal. Horses fighting. Twigs snapping. Then Will's gone.

I gasp, choke on the abundance of air. Scramble to my feet so fast that the edges of my vision darken again, and I nearly pass out. I wrap my arms around a poplar tree, my whole body heaving with each inhalation. I can't get enough air. My pants are wet. I've pissed myself.

Will is rolling on the ground, clutching his side and cursing. Horse rears, strikes Bucky again with his front hooves, and Bucky turns away and kicks defensively with his hind legs.

"Fucking horses," Will roars as he starts to get to his feet. I stagger past him, grab Bucky's reins, and manage to crawl up into the saddle as Will reaches me. With one hand, he grabs my reins close to the bit. Bucky throws his head and I pull on the reins, but Will won't let go. Then he latches onto my left leg with his free hand and tries to pull me down. His mouth is open; he's snarling at me. I can't kick free. I'm going to die here. He's going to pull me down and knock me on the head like a fish.

My reins are so long the ends hang down past Bucky's withers, almost to his legs. Somehow one of them has gotten tangled in my right stirrup. It's been pulled tight by my foot, adding tension to the line. I pull it free.

Then I realize that this is my way out.

I tighten my grip on the rein and lash it across Will's face like a whip. Will screams, paws at his eyes.

I pound my legs against Bucky's ribs, and he breaks into a run. Horse follows, leaving Will staggering after us.

We reach the road and head north. For home. Over the hill, past the cemetery. When I was a kid, I'd always try to hold my breath when we drove past graveyards. Now I'm gasping for air.

I'm leaning over Bucky's neck, trying to urge him on. Bucky stretches out, his stride long and fast, gobs of foam from his mouth flying back. Horse is still following us, sometimes running in front of us, sometimes dropping back as he crow-hops, as though this is all a game. A friendly race.

Right before we reach Dad's driveway, there's an explosion of thunder and lightning, and buckets of rain drop from the sky. Horse jumps sideways, slamming into us. Bucky stumbles, and for a moment I'm afraid he'll go down again. But he steadies himself, and we slow to a trot.

I turn both horses into the pasture and unsaddle them. Horse immediately takes after Bucky again, and before I can think of what to do, they're both out of my reach. As they run over a hill and out of my sight, I can hear Bucky's shrill neigh.

The dirt is turning to mud. I stand there, still holding the bridles, sickened by the thought of Horse running Bucky through a fence. Feeling weak, I sink to my knees. I dig my hands into the mud, feeling it squish between my fingers. Feel the rain soaking through my hair, running down my skin. Then I notice that I'm still wearing Aunt Bea's wedding ring. I can feel Will's eyes burn into me, his hands around my throat. His spit in my face.

I burrow my hands into the mud and sob.

# CHAPTER TWELVE

I call Jack. I'm having trouble talking, but he knows something is wrong.

"I'll be there, Darby. Just hold on," he says.

I sit on the verandah, waiting. Fluffy is purring on my lap, kneading his claws into my thigh. His warmth is making me sleepy. With a groan, Wilson stretches out by the door. Together we watch the afternoon thunderstorm for what seems like hours.

Jack is driving way too fast for the slick roads. I try to tell him to slow down, that I'm okay. But I can't talk without coughing, and my throat hurts like hell. I almost nod off a couple times, but Jack keeps shaking me awake. I just want to sleep.

We cross the Turtle River just before we hit the highway. As we descend into the river valley, I see Bea's car in the river. She climbs out of the ditch, stands on the side of the muddy grid road. She's shivering and hugging herself. Her eyes shine with tears.

I turn to Jack, ask him to stop so we can help her.

"What?" he asks, not understanding.

I turn back to the window, but Bea's gone.

Something is wrong. My thoughts jump and skitter like young foals, then something clicks.

*Will did this to me.*

*Where is he?*

*What if he's waiting for me in Turtleford?*

Jack half-carries me into the Turtleford hospital. The fluorescent lights and bright clean walls hurt my eyes. I vomit in the hallway. I try to apologize, but my voice isn't working right.

I wonder if I'll be able to sing again.

Dr. de Klerk says I must stay overnight. She's asking me something, but I can't understand what she wants me to say. Her accent is beautiful. I would like to visit South Africa someday. I want to ask her if she likes Canadian accents, but my throat is too sore. And I'm so tired.

Jack is talking to Dr. de Klerk and Lena in a hushed voice. What are they talking about? Why are they looking at me that way? I want to ask them what's wrong, but I'm having trouble staying awake.

Lena is here. She squeezes my left hand.

"Is that a wedding band?" She touches the band on my ring finger. And the band seems to vibrate, sending waves through my body, and my brain is laser-focused.

I try to ask her why she didn't tell the police about Bea. She could have saved me this hell. But my voice is an animal growl.

"What are you saying, Darby?" She leans in.

"Tell them," I snarl. And then all my thoughts fall apart, and I close my eyes.

*I'm standing on the shore of Brightsand, looking at the point of rocks revealed by the drought. It's hot as hell.*

*Where's Luke? I wonder. He was just here, I thought, but I can't see him anywhere.*

*There's a terrible burning stench. Burning wood and smoking garbage.*

*I turn my back on the water. A thick line of smoke rises from the black spruce. The red water in the springs is boiling, like lava.*

*I need to leave now, before the fire spreads and I'm trapped. But the sun, which was just overhead, is setting fast, and the lake is the colour of blood.*

I don't open my eyes at first. I'm not sure where I am. I'm afraid of where I am. But when I open them, I realize I'm in the hospital.

The light hurts. I close my eyes again, open them more slowly, trying to adjust.

There's a woman standing in the door to my room. Bea.

She sees that I'm awake, walks toward me. But no, it's Lena. Lena checking on me. She leans over me.

She's crying. I don't know why she's crying, but I'm angry and afraid. But mostly I'm tired. I close my eyes.

*Fire leaps from spruce top to spruce top like a crazed gymnast. I stand on the point. Trapped, but kept safe by the sand and water and rocks surrounding me. Fire can't burn sand and water and rocks.*

*"Darby. Darby." Someone is calling me. I think it's Jack. Why is he here? Where is he? Is he safe? Is he in the fire?*

*I try to yell his name, try to locate him, but my voice isn't working. I can only groan. He'll never find me.*

*Then there's another noise, but I can't quite make it out at first over the fire's roar. It's a growl, I realize.*

*Something lumbers from the trees. It's hulking and muscular, and it almost waddles. Then it stands up on its hind legs, and I realize it's a bear. The biggest black bear I've ever seen. It claws the air, and its paws are higher than the burning tree tops.*

*Fucking hell.*

*The bear sniffs the air. I try to stay still, hoping he won't see me. But he falls back on all fours and walks toward me with purpose.*

*I back up slowly, down the point. I'm trapped between the bear*

*and water. I don't want to go in the water. It's dark and too still.*
*Like it's waiting for me.*

*But the bear pushes me back until I'm balancing on the very edge*
*of the point. My heels hang over the rocks, dipping into the water.*

*The bear is so close now I can feel each exhale on my forehead.*
*He smells like burning garbage and rancid meat. Vomit burns the*
*back of my throat.*

*He rears up, roars. Rips the stars from the sky, pulls down the*
*moon. As the moon crashes to earth, there's a terrible screeching*
*sound, like twisting metal. And a whistling, louder and louder. The*
*light nearly blinds me.*

*I turn away from the bear and the falling moon and the shriek-*
*ing metal and piercing whistle. I dive into the water, into blackness.*
*Silence.*

Jack is stroking my forehead.

"Do you want water, Darby?" he asks. He holds out a cup.

I sip ice water, but I can hardly swallow. My throat is swollen
fire.

"I was looking for you," I croak. "You're safe."

"What?"

I try to explain, but my eyelids weigh too much.

*I dive as deep as I can. The lake has no bottom. How does the water*
*stay in? I wonder.*

*I dive and dive, and time passes and my lungs smoulder. Gradu-*
*ally the water lightens, and I think it must be dawn, so I push back*
*to the surface. And when I break the water's skin, the sun is rising*
*in the east, right where the fire was, but it's out and the trees have*
*already regrown, like magic.*

*I gasp, and the first lungful of air feels so good, but so painful.*

*There's a zing over my head, and something plops in the water*
*just beyond me. And I turn the other way, and a small aluminum*
*fishing boat sits on the placid water, like a fat pelican.*

*I can't make out who's in the boat at first. A man and four kids.*
*And then I realize it's Will, and Luke and Jen and Sam. And a*
*little girl with black hair, streaked red by the sun. Me.*
*They're in danger, I think. I'm in danger.*
*I yell and yell, but no sound comes out, and the water flows into*
*my mouth and down my throat. I start to swim toward them but*
*something is pulling at my legs.*
*Fishing line. I'm tangled in fishing line.*
*It wraps around my legs, cutting my thighs and quads and calves.*
*It's dragging me down.*
*I kick at it and try to pull it off, but the line wraps around my*
*fingers and hands and arms, and soon I'm trussed like a chicken*
*and sinking. And as I descend below the water line, young Darby*
*sees me. Her eyes are big and white, her mouth an O. I stare into*
*her frightened eyes as long as I can. Then all I can see is her chin,*
*her neck, then the silver boat.*
*And finally, there is only dark blue water.*

I'm in the hospital. Why am I in the hospital?

It's late afternoon, I think. The light coming through the
window is strong.

I've been in this room before. I recognize the still life of red
tulips across from my bed. When have I been here?

I close my eyes. Gather my thoughts. It's like herding cats.

Bea was here once. Not long ago. Maybe two years. Head
injury. Something happened when she and Will were moving
yearlings. Her green horse spooked, she said.

But it was a lie. I know now it was a lie.

I open my eyes.

Dad is sitting by my bed. He's wearing the same jeans and
faded blue T-shirt from the day before. I smell sweat and horse
and greasy bear.

He sees I'm awake, takes my left hand. Glances at Bea's wedding band. I pull my hand away.

Dad looks at the band again, and an unspoken question pushes his eyebrows together and up.

*No one around here tells me anything, so why the fuck should I talk?* I think. I tuck my hand under the blanket, and he studies his own hands. Fingernails black with dirt.

But silence is deadly.

"Bea's. It was around his neck," I whisper, my voice a rasp on metal.

Dad closes his eyes for several seconds. When he opens them again, he won't meet my eye. Then I realize he's staring at the door.

I turn my head slowly. Sergeant Steele is standing there, her mouth a straight horizontal line, worry lining her forehead.

"We need to talk," she says. "We don't have him yet. We'll get him, but we need your help."

I clench my hands, touch Bea's wedding band. I pull at it, trying to slide it from my swollen finger. I have to work at it, but it finally pulls free.

I clutch it in the palm of my hand. It's hard and cold. Smooth as a water-worn stone.

If I kept it, I could carry it with me everywhere to remember her, remember what she went through.

"Darby? Can you talk?" she asks.

I touch my throat.

Steele is looking at me, trying to catch my eye. Dad is looking at me, too. I look him in the eye, and he nods.

"Are you ready, Darby?" Steele asks.

"Yes," I whisper.

I open my hand, hold out the ring to Steele.

# PERMISSIONS

# ACKNOWLEDGEMENTS

To my friend and mentor Edna Alford, who saw the novel in the original sliver of a story years ago and later guided me through the revisions. Thank you for your insight into the writing process and all the other wonderful conversations we've had.

To my husband, Corey Parmenter, for sharing his musician's mind and supporting me through this marathon. I love you.

To Bill Kresowaty, one of my early mentors and one of the early readers of this manuscript. Thank you for telling me years ago that I didn't have to grow up in a major city to be a writer.

To my dad for teaching me to ride and read horses. And to my mom for giving this book her blessing even though everyone is going to think she is the controversial mother figure in this book (she's not).

To Leslie Vermeer, Matt Bowes, and Paul Matwychuk at NeWest Press. You've been lovely to work with on this book. I wish such a positive experience for every author.

To Susan Swan, my mentor at the Humber College Creative Writing by Correspondence program. Thank you for showing me how to set down the bones and get closer to the story.

To the Saskatchewan Writers' Guild writing colony at St. Peter's Abbey in Muenster, SK, for the space and time to work through a major revision.

To the people who read earlier versions and offered encouragement, thank you. In particular, thank you Fred and Jackie Helgeton, JacQueline Keller, and Alexis Kienlen for your insight.

To my wonderful crew of friends in this community. You're like family. Thanks for all the book club meetings and kitchen parties and summer afternoons at Brightsand Lake.

To my friend Marleen Conacher, who is both deeply loyal and an independent thinker. Everyone should have such a friend.

To my grandmother, Mary Guenther, for the stories about Anne Boleyn. I still miss you all the time.

**LISA GUENTHER** is a writer and agricultural journalist based in Livelong, Saskatchewan. Her writing has appeared in *Grainews* and *Country Guide*, and she is currently the president of the Canadian Farm Writers' Federation. *Friendly Fire* is her first novel.